Time Travel Sux

Tish Westbury

ISBN: 978-0-244-47159-0

PublishNation
www.publishnation.co.uk

Acknowledgements

Thanks to Danny.

Special thanks to Keith for helping to polish the 1970s.

Cover design conceived by Beth and Tish Westbury, and realised by Jonathan Boothroyd.

Wraparound cover by Scott Gaunt.

Chapter 1.

Myrtle and Maud trudged up the slight incline towards their destination. Loosely described as cleaning ladies, they carried with them the tools of their trade - numerous brushes, various bottles containing lethal liquids designed to eradicate germs with just a squirt, and a mop - all shoved into a battered steel bucket.

They were both feeling the strain of their exertion, as were their lungs, not helped by the autumnal nip in the air or the fact that they were both puffing away on rolled up cigarettes, which dangled inelegantly from the corner of their mouths.

Only last night they had been sitting in the pub, enjoying a quick half after work, bemoaning the fact that life had well and truly passed them by. And this daily stagger to work only served to reinforce this assessment. They had consoled themselves, over another quick half, with the knowledge that during the war they had both done their bit; Maud having served as a driver in the ATS and Myrtle having served endless cups of tea in the NAAFI.

Their destination - the Thurrock factory - had also seen better days. The passage of time had taken its toll and the once pristine London brick structure was sagging under the heavy burden of its Victorian heritage. Like Myrtle and Maud it had done its bit for the war effort, having been converted into a munitions factory for the duration. But now in the groovy, vibrant, way-out modern England of the 1960s it looked… well, knackered, which nicely mirrored Myrtle and Maud's current situation.

'Phew!' puffed Myrtle, the slightly older of the pair who, if you were to see in the street, you would immediately guess was a cleaning lady, mainly because of the bucket but also her attire which was dominated by a wrap-round floral pinny, comfy shoes and topped off by a neatly knotted headscarf.

Ditto Maud. Only she was shorter and more amply proportioned, as she liked to describe herself.

'Huff!' exclaimed Myrtle, 'I wish my Sid could drop us off a bit closer.'

Maud, also out of breath, puffed on her cigarette and gasped, 'I reckon it's his idea of keep-fit, silly bugger. And why does me bucket get heavier every day?'

'I have the same problem with me handbag. It's one of the great mysteries of life, love.'

At that moment they both stopped dead in their tracks. There, within spitting distance, was the oddest sight; especially at seven-thirty in the morning outside the Thurrock factory. A glamorous lady and a handsome gent appeared to be preparing to have a picnic at the front of a rather snazzy sports car.

'Oh, look at those two. They look like they should be up the Kings Road,' marvelled Maud. 'Nice sports car though.'

They edged closer.

Molly, the glamorous lady, opened the picnic basket she had placed on the bonnet of her car. 'Fortunately, I packed a light supper, which judging by the position of the sun is going to be a light breakfast.'

Definitely odd.

'Ah, smoked salmon and champagne,' said James, the handsome gent, appreciatively.

Myrtle and Maud edged even closer, trying not to appear nosey but failing miserably.

James looked up. 'Good morning, ladies. What lovely weather.' He smiled and then looked into the far distance across the fields that overlooked the factory; an intermittent glint of light had caught his eye.

'Morning,' replied Myrtle, undeterred by the gent's sudden lack of interest; she had that effect on most men these days. 'Nice weather for a champagne breakfast, eh?'

'Indeed,' Molly concurred. 'Perhaps you'd care to join **us**?' She emphasised the "us" hoping that it would encourage James to stop being so impolite. After all, Debrett's guides on etiquette dominated his library. But to no avail.

'Thanks ever so, but we've got to keep a clear head,' said Maud.

Molly looked surprised. 'Really?'

'Aye, Maud's right. We've got lots of cleaning to do, you see.'
Myrtle jiggled her bucket, which obligingly clanged.

'Ah, I see,' Molly said, not really seeing but thinking each to their
own.

'Well, ta-ra!' said Maud, picking up her bucket.

'Goodbye,' said Molly. She watched the ladies as they headed
towards the factory. 'Do you think we should have warned them about
the time machine, James?'

'What?' said James, returning his attention back to his colleague.

'The, um, oh…I've forgotten. How strange.'

Myrtle and Maud made their way towards the small door housed
in the large wooden warehouse doors - their preferred route to work
because it was the closest and led directly to the place with which they
had the strongest affinity: a small area tucked away in the corner of
the warehouse which had comfy chairs and a kettle. Pausing to stub
out their cigarettes, they stepped through the tiny door with some
difficulty. Myrtle often wondered why the door was only really
suitable for a small person carrying absolutely nothing, but today her
mind was on other things.

'Oh! Wasn't that chap dashing?' she trilled as they both plonked
their buckets down. 'And he had an air of mystery about him.'

'Yes! Ohh, he could whisk me off in his sports car any day.'

Had they not been getting carried away, they might have noticed
that they had put their buckets down on two circular mats which,
although they looked perfectly at home in the 1960s - one being black
and the other white: very stylish and Mary Quant - they were totally
out of place on the gnarled wooden floor of the Thurrock warehouse.
But Myrtle and Maud were too busy getting carried away!

'And champagne at seven-thirty in the morning,' said Myrtle,
aghast. 'How the other half live, eh?'

''Course I don't like champagne m'self, makes me a bit burpy. I
prefer a nice stout.'

'I had noticed,' said Myrtle, smiling as she thought of Maud's love
of a stout or two and the resulting raucous behaviour, which invariably
ended in Maud doing her famous imitation of Gracie Fields (albeit in
a Yorkshire accent). 'And that lady seemed very nice. I thought she
was going to be all superior and la-dee-da but she was lovely.'

'Really lovely,' agreed Maud. 'Mind, I'm not so sure about that trendy trouser suit she was wearing.'

'I know, it's all very well being fab and with-it, but not much use when you're in our line of work,' Myrtle stated, pulling one of the chairs out from under the table and flopping down into it.

'Aye, totally impractical for sitting around with your feet up having a cuppa.' Maud crossed over to the small tea-making area. 'Talking of cuppas, I'll put the kettle on.'

Myrtle pulled out another chair and rested her legs on it, hoping that her varicose veins wouldn't give her too much gyp today. She pulled a paperback book and her reading specs out of one of her pockets and put them on the table. Reading was a habit instilled into her by her mother, Ethel, who'd never read a book in her life and had ended up married to a wastrel. Certain that these two facts were linked and determined that the same fate shouldn't befall her daughter, she'd encouraged Myrtle to "get down to the library and read something, or it will all end in tears, my girl." After a few false starts Myrtle had found that she enjoyed reading books by someone called Jane Austen and some sisters known collectively as the Brontës, recognised by many people at the time as the nearest equivalent to marriage guidance. This course of action succeeded, in that Myrtle had ended up married to a lovable rogue and could wile away hours at work reading. But first she and Maud had to wile away a bit of time having a good old natter over a cup of tea.

Maud filled the kettle, plugged it back into the wall socket and flicked the switch.

In the opposite corner to where Maud was pottering around, a white metal object with two integral lids on the top gently hummed into life. Its readout panel flickered.

Maud tutted as she threw away an empty wine bottle which had been left in the sink; she really must have a word with the night security blokes about being more subtle with their midnight drinking. Then she started chatting away as she got back on track and rummaged around for the teapot and caddy. 'This cleaning job's always been a cushy number and no doubt.'

'Aye, and thankfully things seem to be settling down after the hoo-ha over those poisoned envelopes.'

'What a palaver! I don't think I'll ever be able to lick an envelope again.' Maud, having placed everything she'd need on the tea tray, paused briefly and her attention was finally drawn to the white metal object, which was now vibrating and buzzing slightly. 'Here, look at that.'

Myrtle glanced over. Her eyes widened and she leapt to her feet. 'Oh, it looks like one of them twin-tub washing machines I've been pestering my Sid to buy me,' she said, rushing over to join Maud, who had wandered towards the machine. 'Mrs Owen at number 91's got one.'

'They're a bit pricey, aren't they?'

'Worth their weight in gold, I'd say.' Her eyes shone. 'Just think of it - I could throw away my washing board and mangle… bliss!'

Maud leant forward and, at random, pressed one of the buttons on the readout panel; in unison the two lids sprang open. She peered inside and was surprised to see a weird electronic apparatus housed inside each of the tubs; they were whirling around creating sizzling, blue sparks which darted in all directions inside the drums.

Myrtle, alerted by Maud's silence, leant over and peered into the machine, which had started shaking with energy. 'Never seen anything like that before.'

Maud turned her attention to the readout panel with its buttons and dials. 'This must be the heat selector,' she guessed, twisting the dial. The panel read 11:10:1987.

Annoyed with herself that she'd left her reading specs on the table, Myrtle peered at the panel then moved her head back so she could read the display. 'That doesn't make sense.'

'It's very sophisticated,' reasoned Maud.

Suddenly the noise coming from the machine went up a gear and the humming became a whining. The machine started to rattle.

Myrtle grabbed at Maud and pulled her away. 'Don't like the look of that,' she shouted over the din. 'Best get back.'

'Here, that orange button's gone green. I wonder what will happen if I press it?'

'I wouldn't,' instructed Myrtle, 'my Sid says never go near a machine if you don't know how it works.'

Maud briefly wondered why Myrtle always paid so much heed to her Sid and then, with a mischievous look in her eye, she darted forward and stabbed at the button.

Two funnels of swirling, bright blue light shot up out of the tubs, arched over Maud (who ducked) and landed on the two groovy mats enveloping their buckets. Maud, now at eye level with the readout panel, shouted to Myrtle, 'It says prepare for transit!'

'Glory! Quick get back, love!' Myrtle yelled, waving frantically at her friend.

Maud felt a sizzle of energy on her back and, on hearing an odd whoosh-wash sound, she turned round just as the swirling beams of light intensified and the mats, along with their buckets, started to vanish. 'Blimey!' she exclaimed, reaching out to grab her mop.

'Just leave it!' beseeched Myrtle.

'But it's me lucky mop,' she cried, taking hold of the handle. An odd sensation of weightlessness floated through her body. 'Ohh,' she uttered, and vanished into the beam.

'Maud?!' yelled Myrtle. 'Oh heck, I can see this is going to be a right-old day.' And with that she grabbed her mop and closed her eyes. 'Ohh,' she uttered as she too vanished.

Chapter 2.

Located at an indeterminable point in time and space is the, some would say, aptly-named PLOTLINE monitoring station. Its primary function being to Protect the Legitimate, Official Time Line - or in other words, keep the historic flow of events, as officially recognised, on the right track.

Who or what entity decides the official legitimacy of the timeline has been subject to many theories and in-depth discussions amongst the higher-brained species in the myriad of universes that make up the Multiverse, causing much speculation and controversy. But interestingly they all came to, will come to, are coming to the same conclusion - that it probably has something to do with beings in grey suits, who may or may not be part of the mysterious group known variously as the Illuminati, the Astralati and the Novrati. Not to be muddled with the Literati, the Glitterati or the Arti-Farti.

One such theorist, the Xa of Sands, who was the first being to notice the delicious juxtaposition between the two crucial elements contained in the conclusion: the dull and the bright, proceeded to make obscene amounts of money by writing endless books on the subject. Only to eventually reveal that the truth could only be exposed if everyone in the Multiverse removed their sunglasses. (Which didn't go down very well with her readers, especially the ones who had decided to stop wearing sunglasses and got terrible frown lines).

Fortunately, the keeping-an-eye-on-it bit is handled by massive computers, thus saving a colossal workforce the tedious task of staring endlessly at computer-generated holographic images of oscillating lines looking for the slightest glitch. Which, of course, would be impossible; especially if one was trying to drink a cup of tea.

Predictably Myrtle and Maud's unexpected incursion into the nebulous strata of time activated the PLOTLINE monitoring system thus: an insistent alarm sounded and the banks of computer screens (the current designer was going through a retro phase) flashed up the word ALERT and a soothing voice reiterated the sentiment.

'Alert,' it said to no-one in particular because, let's face it, every sentient being in this particular universe with any sense and the ability to do so had probably gone to make a cup of tea, thereby making damn sure that they didn't get roped into any PLOTLINE monitoring. Undeterred the voice continued, 'PLOTLINE monitoring system activated. Detecting fluctuations in the Wave of Temporalati. Time travel confirmed,' it purred. 'Origin: the 11th of October 1965. Destination: the 11th of October 1987. Categorised as level five incursion. Monitoring system on standby.' The alarm stopped and STANDBY flashed up on the ubiquitous screens.

As Myrtle travelled through time she was sure she could hear someone calling her name and, as bizarre as it may seem, she could hear herself calling to someone whose name was Ohhh-ahhh!

Cognitive confusion, especially for the first-time time traveller, is well documented and is explained by the curious nature of the reaction caused by excited matter (cytrinos), colliding with lazy matter (in this instance cleaning ladies and their buckets). A further by-product of time travel is a temporal boom, which is created when the mixture of excited and lazy matter reaches a critical mass interaction point and there's a loud boom. (It is interesting to note that many beings believe that the temporal boom is a faint echo of the Big Bang, renamed by these beings as the not-so-catchy Say Goodbye to Your Eardrums Bang).

Myrtle, now officially a member of the time travellers club, felt the strange sensation of weightlessness being replaced by the strangely familiar sensation of not-weightlessness and she opened her eyes. In front of her was a delighted Maud, who rushed towards her mouthing something that she couldn't quite catch. Myrtle gently shook her head and felt her eardrums pop. She took a deep breath, released the steel-like grip she had on her mop, and swayed slightly.

Maud put a steadying arm around her and guided her to the nearest chair. 'You take the weight off, love, and I'll find the kettle,' she shouted into Myrtle's ear. 'It's very odd; everything looks brighter somehow.'

Myrtle pulled a duster from out of her pocket and dabbed at her brow. She gazed at the whitewashed walls. 'That reminds me, I must remember to get a pint of milk on my way home.'

Maud ambled around in an ineffective manner, clearly still adjusting to her bizarre experience; which she was trying to pass off as a funny turn. She had opened and closed the top two drawers of one of the filing cabinets before realising she'd forgotten what she was looking for. Undaunted, she tottered up the short corridor, past the stairwells which led up to the offices, to the factory floor. She opened the main doors and, to her astonishment, the antiquated machines which lovingly churned out envelopes were gone, replaced by huge shiny monster-machines which spewed out reams of lined paper. The pervading smell of glue had been replaced by the powerful aroma of ink. She slammed the door shut and then opened it again. She stood there desperately trying to make sense of it all. Then Myrtle appeared at her side. They looked at each other, agog.

'It's…' croaked Maud.

'Completely…changed,' yelled Myrtle.

They backed away slowly and then bolted, grabbing their buckets as they made a dash for the warehouse door. After a relatively speedy exit from the warehouse, helped by their overwhelming desire to get the hell out of there, Myrtle and Maud's initial relief turned to yet more astonishment. They'd almost managed to convince themselves that they'd both had a funny turn, and for some reason couldn't remember the complete modernisation of the Thurrock factory, but they couldn't ignore the irrefutable evidence before them. The street which lead up to the factory was generally empty and quiet; the workforce either walked or cycled to work, except for the interim managing director who drove a clapped-out Jag. But now it was lined with parked cars and clusters of small buildings of a uniform design splayed out where once open fields had stretched as far as the eye could see. A young woman wearing the most outlandish outfit they'd ever seen tottered past on white stilettos, followed by a waft of overpowering perfume. There was an odd feeling in the air - a kind of tingling frisson of energy.

Maud was the first to be able to engage her vocal capacity. 'What's going on?'

Myrtle was staring at the swish new sign installed on the side of the warehouse, which read: THURROCK'S CONTINUOUS STATIONARY. Her brain was struggling to come up with a remotely plausible, if flimsy, explanation when she heard a voice.

'Oy! You two!'

They turned and saw a young man dressed in an ill-fitting suit and a garish tie striding towards them. They exchanged a puzzled glance. What now?

'At last,' exclaimed the young man. 'You're late, yah. I am trying to run a business you know.'

'Late? For what?' enquired Myrtle.

'You are here for the last-minute cleaning job up town, aren't you? Yah.'

'Why does he keep saying "yah"?' Maud whispered to Myrtle.

'Lord knows.'

The man glared at them. 'Well, if my two pounds an hour rate isn't good enough…'

'Two pounds an hour!' Myrtle blurted out, louder then she'd intended.

The man, mistaking Myrtle's astonishment for indignation, focused more keenly on the two women. Obviously, he'd underestimated their grasp of supply and demand economics. He held his hands up in a conciliatory fashion. 'OK yah, two pounds ten then, but only because you bear a passing resemblance to our wonderful Prime Minister.'

Myrtle and Maud's jaws dropped.

Suddenly the device he was clutching made a weird beeping sound. 'Excuse me.' He pressed a button on the keypad and started talking into it. 'Hi yah, Roger here…' He wandered off.

'Well, of all the nerve! I've never been so offended in all my days! We don't look like Harold Wilson, do we?' said Myrtle, staring at Maud and trying to picture her in a raincoat, smoking a pipe, droning on about politics.

'Well, he certainly knows how to make you feel good about yourself,' said Maud sarcastically. 'Still,' her tone softened to a reverent hush, 'two pounds ten an hour, that's er…fifty shillings an hour! We could do a day's work and retire.'

Myrtle nodded. 'Aye, it's amazing.' She looked over at Roger. 'Here, what's that brick he's talking into?'

'Looks like one of them army radio-telephone type thingies to me,' she replied. She waved enthusiastically at Roger. 'Yoo-hoo!' she called. 'Two pounds ten sounds fine.'

Roger did a thumbs-up sign, said something into his brick and beckoned the ladies towards his minibus. As they pottered over, Maud nudged her pal. 'Here, Myrtle, you'll be able to get one of them twin-tubs.'

'Hmm, I've gone right off the idea.'

Chapter 3.

As they weaved their way through the traffic, Maud sat staring into space, doing a lot of mental arithmetic and counting numbers on her fingers. The odd "oh" and "ah" escaped her lips.

Myrtle was staring out of the window, lost in thought. She was trying to make sense of the strange sights all around her; the only problem was that she kept getting distracted by the vision of shillings shimmering into her mind. She glanced at Roger's reflection in the rearview mirror, then it hit her: all the bizarre events that she and Maud had experienced before they'd met Roger had been relegated to the overactive imagination section of her mind by a sudden flood of greedy impulses, but where had these impulses come from? She closed her eyes and replayed recent events in her mind, and she realised that it was Roger's initial offer of two pounds an hour that had activated the greed override switch in her brain. Forcing herself to focus on events prior to this, the numbers displayed on the twin-tub washing machine's readout panel flashed into her mind's eye: 1-9-8-7. Her eyes shot open. Bingo! She looked over at Maud, who still appeared to be in the thrall of the idea of becoming stinking rich, leant towards her and whispered, 'You thinking about how to spend all that money, love?'

Maud smiled. 'That obvious, is it?'

'Well… aye, but listen…' Her tone darkened. 'I don't think we're in 1965 anymore.'

'*Not in 1965*!' exclaimed Maud.

Roger glanced at them in the rearview mirror.

'Shh,' instructed Myrtle.

'Where else can we be?'

Myrtle leant even closer. '1987. Remember the readout panel.'

'Heck.'

'Makes sense; that's why all the cars and people look so…odd.'

'Oh aye,' said Maud, peering out of the window. 'Who on earth thinks outrageously large shoulder pads and big shaggy hair is a good look?'

'Most of the population, by the look of it.'

The two ladies stared out of the windows, contemplating the enormity of Myrtle's revelation. The more they thought about it the more enormous it became.

So overwhelming that Maud, for one, decided to stop thinking about it altogether and ask the obvious question: 'What should we do?'

She was confident that her generally wiser friend would somehow know what to do when you find yourself in the future.

Myrtle, who was still struggling with the enormity of it all, gave her a blank look.

'Myrtle, what now?'

Myrtle looked at her pal. How should she know? She'd never bothered to read 'The Time Machine' by H.G Wells, preferring the more, as she thought at the time, useful novels of Austen and the Brontës. Which, as she thought about it, was ridiculous; even in her youth she'd never met a chap as deep and brooding as Mr. Darcy or Heathcliff. The chaps she met were just keen on a quick cuppa at the Lyons teahouse followed by a bit of how's your father. But she knew Maud was depending on her, so she went for the most obvious solution. 'Let's stick with it for now.'

'You mean - do the job, take the money, and run?'

Myrtle nodded.

'Alright, ladies, this is it,' called Roger. He pulled over, jumped out and opened the back doors for Myrtle and Maud. They clambered out of the minibus and looked around. Myrtle once again felt the strange frisson of energy hit her, sizzling up her nerve endings; the kind of feeling you get when you only need one dratted number on the bingo.

Roger handed them their buckets. 'This way, yah.' He led them towards the barred entrance to an underground station, unlocked the padlock and heaved the metal grille open. 'I need you to clear a pathway on the southbound platform, some filming bods are coming along later to do a recce, or whatever they call it. I told them the Strand station would be a better idea, but hey, what do I know? Shouldn't take you long, I'll be in Bertie's Wine Bar, yah.'

'What's a wine bar?' enquired Maud.

'A posh boozer,' Roger informed her.

'Oh, right. Aren't you going to show us the way?' she asked, peering into the gloomy, unappealing ticket hall and thinking any kind of boozer, even a posh one, would be very welcome right now.

Roger smiled. 'Just follow the signs, OK? The main power switch is inside on the left.' He handed Myrtle a torch. 'Take this just in case.'

Myrtle pressed the button on the handle and checked the light - nothing. She held it upside down and shook it, which produced a dim light; she shook it a bit harder and the full beam came on.

Roger rummaged around in his jacket pocket and pulled out a set of keys, which he passed to Maud. 'Spare keys for the bus in case you need any extra cleaning stuff.' And with that he started stabbing at the keypad on his brick and strode off.

'Ta love,' called Maud.

Myrtle watched him leave, unimpressed. 'Well, he's about as much use as a used tea bag.'

Maud shuddered. 'Ohh, I can't be doing with them. Too modern for my liking. Besides, my Herbie gets a bit miffed when I tear them open for my tea leaf readings.'

The beam of the torch pierced into the dark recesses of the ticket hall, throwing up spooky shadows. Mysterious shapes loomed out of the darkness as Myrtle, closely followed by Maud - who was clinging onto her friend - tentatively edged their way into the, frankly smelly, environs of the station.

'Quick, love, find the blessed light switch.' Maud's voice quivered as she heard a faint scurrying noise close by. 'Fifty shillings an hour, fifty shillings an hour,' she muttered.

Myrtle directed the torch onto the wall to their left. 'Ah, there it is.' She passed her bucket to Maud, grasped hold of the industrial lever and yanked it down. The lights flickered on and the gentle whirring and clanking of the lift mechanism activating floated towards them. 'Come on, this way,' said Myrtle, pocketing the torch and taking back her bucket. She guided her friend deeper into the abandoned ticket hall.

'I hope there aren't too many rats down here.' Maud hated rats.

'More likely to be mice,' remarked Myrtle, as she thumbed the lift button.

'Oh, no! I can't stand mice.' Maud scanned the immediate area around her feet and dashed into the lift as soon as the large metal door slid open.

Myrtle pressed the illuminated button and the doors closed.

Maud relaxed slightly. 'How come you know your way around?'

Myrtle glanced furtively over Maud's shoulder and lowered her voice to a whisper, 'I worked here during the war.'

Maud looked confused. 'But I thought you worked for the NAAFI.'

'That was a smokescreen; I worked here when it was used by the War Cabinet as a top secret base.'

Maud looked impressed. 'You don't mean to say that we're walking in the footsteps of Churchill? God rest his soul.'

'Aye, quite something, eh?'

The lift clunked to a halt and the doors slid open. The ladies stepped out and Myrtle ushered Maud down the grimy tile-lined passage lit by a string of light bulbs, which jiggled as a tube train whizzed through the disused station.

'You mean you worked for Churchill?' asked Maud with a touch of awe in her voice.

'Well, I made him the odd cuppa. He even once told me that I made a fine cup of tea,' said Myrtle, brimming with pride.

'Blimey, you kept that quiet!'

'It was all very hush-hush, but I reckon I can tell you now we're in the 1980s,' explained Myrtle.

They had reached the platform; the area beyond the edge had been bricked up and the decaying remnants of a warren of rooms running off a central corridor stretched out in front of them.

'Is that it?' said a disappointed Maud.

'Here, why don't we have a quick peek into the top-top secret base?'

'How can a base be top-top secret?' asked Maud.

'By being a top secret base hidden inside a top secret base, that's how.' Myrtle plonked her bucket down and stared intently at a mucky Art Deco'esque NO EXIT sign on the wall. She took out her mop and used it to press the centre of the O. Nothing happened. 'Must be the other one,' she said. They picked their way down the debris-strewn central corridor, avoiding upturned chairs, the occasional rusting metal frame of a bunk bed, and even the odd battered enamel mug. Myrtle once more pressed the O on an identical sign and, after a series of clunks, a hidden door swung open.

'Cor! What a stench!' exclaimed Maud. She rooted out her duster from her pinny and clasped it to her nose.

Myrtle leant her mop against the platform wall, took the torch out of her pocket, switched it on, shook it and shone the beam into the dark passage. 'Oh, I feel all young and foolish again.' And with that she was off.

Maud, who was not altogether convinced that going into a secret passage in a disused underground station was a good idea, put her bucket down and then, with a shrug of her shoulders, followed her friend.

'Now if memory serves… it's this way,' Myrtle joked, pointing down the corridor - the only route possible.

The rumble of an approaching tube train gathering pace reverberated down the corridor and, with a whoosh, warm air forced its way past Myrtle and Maud, making discarded papers flutter around their ankles.

'Hang on!' said Myrtle. They were now level with a large, rusty metal door, which had NO UNAUTHORISED ENTRY emblazoned on it. 'I always wanted to have a look down here.' Passing the torch to Maud, she slid the large bolts back with surprising ease - a fact she might have found suspicious, had she not been reliving her glory days - and slowly heaved open the heavy door.

'What's down there?' enquired Maud nervously, realising that her old friend had a reckless streak that she'd hitherto hidden exceptionally well.

'A network of inter-linking tunnels was the rumour. They had emergency tunnels all over the place back then. Some said you could get to Buckingham Palace.'

'Well, I never did!'

Myrtle finally got the door open and the two ladies were surprised to see an eerie, green glow infusing the passage. They felt a sudden chill in the air. They snuck through the door, only to stop abruptly when a weird, unearthly wail drifted towards them.

'What…was…that?' stammered Maud.

'Let's find out.'

'Let's not,' said Maud, turning to go. But Myrtle was off. Maud watched her receding figure wondering why she hadn't seen any of this in her morning tea leaf reading session. Obviously some things are beyond the capacity of humble tea leaves to predict - time travel being one. 'Botheration,' muttered Maud.

Maud could be surprisingly quick on her feet when she put her mind to it. Of course, she usually put her mind to it when she was rushing to catch the bus to the bingo hall, but she knew she couldn't very well leave Myrtle having a nose around a scary passage on her own, so she scurried down the passageway and caught up with Myrtle, who was saying something about her Sid's favourite television show. '…Very creepy what with all them aliens…' was all Maud caught.

'You're not helping, love,' said Maud, as they turned left down a short passageway heading towards the source of the green glow.

'Oh, sorry.' The weird wail reverberated around the walls. 'This will take your mind off it - fascinating facts about the London Underground.' She paused for effect as a nearby train rattled by. 'Did you know that the ticket hall at Bank station was built in the crypt of a church?'

'Myrtle!'

'Oh, aye.' They paused as they came to the end of the passageway and were confronted with a much larger tunnel, one designed to take the squat trains that service the deeper underground lines. 'Now, this is fascinating - Angel, Manor House and Royal Oak are all named after pubs,' she stated, confident that this particular fact would calm Maud down.

Maud found the mention of her favourite pastime oddly reassuring and felt her anxiety lessening. 'That is interesting. How come you know so much about the Under…' Maud's voice ground to a halt. Through the swirling green mist the outline of a structure began to take shape.

Myrtle and Maud stood there gawping and peered into the green mist.

Maud's knees began to wobble. 'What…?' was all she could manage.

Myrtle, recovering from the shock of finding a green, glowing Nissen hut - which was regularly expelling plumes of steam - nestling under the arch of a tunnel, realised that this had to be the source of the weird wailing and set off towards the structure.

17

Chapter 4.

Bloody freezing was the only way of describing the interior of the Nissen hut.

Having managed to coax Maud up the stairs to the main hatch and prise it open; the combination of the Arctic blast hitting them and the sinister wailing had turned Maud's legs to jelly and she'd sank down onto the stairs, clinging onto the handrail and desperately trying not to keel over. Myrtle had given her a reassuring pat on the shoulder, pulled her own headscarf around her ears and ventured into the hut.

With every breath, Myrtle felt the cold air freezing her nose and throat, reminding her of the first time she'd defrosted Mrs Owen's ice-making compartment in her highly sought-after fridge; not for Myrtle were the delights of frozen fish-fingers. Mrs Owen had instructed her just to leave the fridge door open and let nature take its course, but after a quick flick round the whole house with her duster, followed by a number of cuppas and far too many digestives, Myrtle couldn't take it anymore and she'd grabbed a bread knife, stuck her head into the fridge and started chipping away at the pesky white ice. If memory served, it was only on her third defrosting attempt that she realised she should probably have switched off the fridge first.

Wondering whether she was suffering from the early stages of hypothermia she dragged her mind back into the here-and-now and peered into the murky recesses of the hut, in the general direction of where the sinister wailing seemed to be coming from.

'Yoo-hoo,' she called out softly. The wailing continued, punctuated by a faint rustling sound. As her eyes grew accustomed to the green light she noticed banks of machinery dotted around, with dim lights glowing on the panels. She gently touched one of the nearby panels and to her surprise it was warm to the touch. 'Very odd.'

Suddenly a voice whispered in her ear. 'What's very odd?'

Myrtle shrieked and whirled round to see… 'Maud! Don't do that!'

'Sorry, love, but I was worried about you.' The unearthly wailing intensified. 'Can't imagine why,' she joked.

'You're very chipper all of a sudden.'

'Aye, well, I found a barley sugar in me pocket; I feel a lot better now. It was tucked under my emergency bottle of cleaning liquid; no idea how long it's been there.' She pulled out Roger's torch and shone its feeble light onto the wall by the hatch. 'Now, there must be a light switch somewhere.'

'Not sure if I want to know what's in here with us, love,' muttered Myrtle, as the baleful wailing continued.

Maud shivered. 'Blimey, it is cold in here…oh, that looks hopeful,' she said, and she threw the switch. There was a series of clunks as banks of lights activated.

Myrtle and Maud could now see that they were standing on a gallery overlooking a vast array of glass pods reflecting the soft, golden glow which diffused the structure. As they descended the metal stairs they noticed that the eerie wailing had stopped, but the rustling sound was louder.

Myrtle tentatively approached the nearest pod and wiped the fine layer of ice away. Maud peered over her shoulder. They were both surprised and quite relieved to see a mass of leaves quivering against the glass.

'Blimey,' exclaimed Maud, 'it looks like a giant version of that cheese plant my Herbie gave me for Christmas last year!'

'The romantic devil,' quipped Myrtle, as they both took in the scale of the operation. 'There must be hundreds of them.'

'What are they doing here?' asked Maud, but Myrtle had turned her attention to the area directly under the gallery. A large cylindrical piece of machinery had caught her eye. They approached it cautiously and peered into the small porthole on the side. A secondary tubular structure sat in the centre surrounded by pipes and tubes. Myrtle stepped back and gazed upwards. It rose right up into the gallery.

'What is it?' whispered Maud, not sure why she was whispering but it seemed appropriate.

Myrtle pursed her lips and indicated that they should go back up the stairs.

After a bit of huffing and puffing, and the odd whinge about her varicose veins from Myrtle, they clanged their way back up to the gallery. Myrtle inspected the banks of machinery she had seen earlier and noticed that they were linked by heavy-duty cables to the uppermost section of the large, cylindrical structure housed under their feet.

'What is it?' Maud asked again.

'I think it's a nuclear reactor, not that I've ever seen one in real life.'

'Looks like a giant washing machine to me.'

'You won't want to put your smalls in there, I can tell you,' remarked Myrtle.

Maud wasn't sure what a nuclear reactor was or what it would do to her smalls, but she took her friend's word for it.

'It's very strange,' mused Myrtle, 'a cavernous Nissen hut full of plants, with a nuclear reactor keeping them cold, in a tunnel under Mayfair.'

'Hmm, all this must have been down here for a long time going by all this dust,' said Maud, running a finger over one of the panels and blowing the dust into the atmosphere to prove her point.

'P'raps we'd better give it a quick clean…' Myrtle turned to Maud, astonished. 'I don't think I've ever uttered those words before. To actually want to dust something properly, it's a very odd sensation.'

'It must be because we're getting so well paid,' hazarded Maud. 'Blimey, what with all this exploring we've probably earned about a hundred shillings by now! How many florins is that? Oh, aye, fifty.' She stood there with a contented look on her face as she contemplated what she could possibly spend so much money on. 'Ohh,' she uttered, 'I'm getting a strange urge to buy some British Telecom shares, whatever they are!' Maud felt a shiver run down her spine. 'Heck! Now I'm getting the urge to buy our council flat.'

An incredulous Myrtle stared at Maud. 'What are you on about? That's the most ridiculous thing I've ever heard!'

Maud shrugged her shoulders. 'That time travelling must have scrambled my brains,' she said, pulling her duster out of her pocket.

'Just be careful not to press any buttons, especially if they're green,' instructed Myrtle, whipping out her duster with a flourish.

'Right-ho.'

And they went to work.

To their amazement they both found it very satisfying removing the thick layers of dust to reveal the shiny metallic surface of the readout panels, and it also warmed them up. Maud started humming a jaunty little tune and Myrtle quickly discovered that a bit of spit and polish was highly effective at removing ingrained dust.

Myrtle paused to admire their handiwork just as Maud gave another panel a vigorous wipe; which sent plumes of dust into the air.

'Heck! I think I've pressed a button!' announced Maud, squinting at the lettering she'd just revealed. 'On the primary power grid panel, whatever that is?'

Myrtle looked at her in despair.

'Don't fret, it's not gre… Ohh, it's gone green,' she cried.

'Hell's bells, Maud! When are you going to learn!'

Out of nowhere, a calm, melodic voice pronounced, 'Locking down zone B7.' The bolts on the main hatch slid shut. 'Deactivating containment measures.' This announcement resulted in a lot of hissing and whirling in the pod-storage area.

Myrtle and Maud dashed over to get a decent view. They watched in trepidation. In unison the pod screens rose and a purple light shone down on each of the plants, making them quiver wildly. Myrtle and Maud waited on tenterhooks for further useful, if somewhat complex, information from the disembodied voice, but with none forthcoming Myrtle started edging towards the stairs.

Maud grabbed her arm, 'I don't think that's a good idea, love.'

'I want to take a closer look.'

Myrtle and Maud reached the metal walkway between the pods.

'Reanimation of life-forms commencing,' the voice informed them.

Craning their necks, they both tip-toed towards the nearest bank of pods. A sudden gush of water cascaded down onto the plants, drenching Myrtle and Maud in the process. They shrieked. Then a sudden blast of warm, humid air caught them before they'd even had the chance to stop shrieking.

Finally their shrieks petered out, and for a few of seconds Myrtle and Maud stood there looking like drowned rats. Then, to their amazement, the plants started unfurling themselves out of their pods.

'Glory,' exclaimed Myrtle.

Maud grimaced and wisely saved her breath for yet another strenuous clamber up the stairs.

Myrtle made it to the main hatch first and was frantically wrestling with one of the large bolts, which refused point-blank to budge. 'For crying out loud!'

Maud joined her, bobbing around in an agitated manner.

Suddenly they heard a beeping noise coming from the other side of the hatch.

'Releasing locking mechanism on primary hatch,' the calm voice informed them. The bolts slid back and with a hiss the hatch swung open.

Two figures loomed out of the dissipating greeny-purple mist.

Myrtle and Maud backed away.

The two figures stepped into the gallery.

'Hmm, Maud?'

'Aye.'

'Can you see two chaps dressed in suits and bowler hats, standing right in front of us?'

'Aye.'

'Oh, good,' said Myrtle, relieved.

The two men stared impassively at them.

Myrtle took a step towards them. 'HELP!' she implored them.

'You have activated the reanimation process,' stated one of the po-faced men, as he strode past them and scanned the pod-storage area.

A wary Myrtle eyed the other man, who was barring their escape route. 'You know about all this then?'

'We are the guardians of the plants, programmed to protect and nourish them. I am designated Unit Two and that is Unit One,' he said, pointing at his partner.

'So you're like gardeners then?' said Maud. 'They look more like bank managers to me,' she muttered.

Myrtle studied the two men. Their words had a familiar ring about them - where had she heard them before? Then she remembered: on her Sid's favourite television show. 'They're robots!'

'Correct,' stated Unit One, who had finished surveying the scene below and was proceeding to study the control panels on the primary power grid.

'What's all this in aid of?' asked Myrtle.

Unit Two stared at the two humans, assessing the level of intelligence displayed and calculating the level of information to impart. The unit concluded that, on the evidence of its visual input devices, these two humans must be intelligent - they had reanimated the plants, after all. So it said, 'When our E-type plasma sphere reached the Omega stage of imminent gravitational core collapse, our primary mission was to convey the hibernating life forms contained in this cryogenic stasis chamber to a new biosphere…'

'Hold up,' said Myrtle, not sure if she could take any more nonsense, 'I'd rather you didn't clog up our brains with a load of cobblers; just give us a basic thumbnail sketch, if you'd be so kind.'

After a brief pause to compute what cobblers were and what a thumbnail sketch was, Unit Two continued. 'Acknowledged. Retrieving salient information. Our interstellar craft landed on your planet, but a disruption to the power grid led to a command failure in the reanimation process.'

Myrtle glanced across at Maud, who had abandoned any attempt to understand the incomprehensible stream of words coming from the robot and looked like she was having a stultifying flashback to her school days. Then Myrtle noticed that both the robots were staring at her, presumably waiting for her response. 'Hmm, I s'pose that was short and sweet,' she said, 'but a bit too complicated for my liking.'

Unit Two immediately encoded its earlier flawed assessment of the two humans into its databank reserved for complications relating to the assessment of alien life forms' intelligence. 'Acknowledged. Temporarily decreasing I.Q. of this unit to assist communication.' This was a measure rarely used by the units. However, on this strange planet it had come in very handy on more than one occasion. 'Comparative intelligence determined,' the unit stated and in a flash its face became animated. 'The long and short of it, getting down to the nitty-gritty: our planet was about to blow up, so we had to find a new home for this lot.' Unit Two waved in the general direction of the storage pods. 'Your planet looked nice so we landed here but didn't have a clue on how to wake up the plants.'

'Ohh.' Myrtle didn't like the sound of that. In fact, she was beginning to get a nasty feeling in the pit of her stomach; the kind of feeling she got when she saw an exceptionally gruesome toilet that needed her attention. A feeling that could be guaranteed to be eased by a nice cuppa; fat chance of that, she thought.

'Thanks for that,' said Unit Two. The unit grasped Maud's hand and shook it firmly.

Maud smiled. 'Well, we're glad we could help, aren't we, Myrtle?'

'Hmm,' muttered Myrtle, wishing that a dirty lavvy was all she had to worry about right now.

Suddenly Unit One, who had been standing there all po-faced throughout the exchange, reached into its breast pocket and pulled out a matt-silver coloured object. An object that definitely wasn't one of those army radio-type thingies that Roger seemed to be so attached to. In fact, it resembled a gun. 'We must eliminate all threats to the life forms.'

'Oh dear, that sounds like hard work. I hope you're getting well paid,' said Maud.

Through clenched teeth Myrtle said, 'He means us!'

'Glory!'

Myrtle sighed and adopted a casual manner, which involved leaning against a nearby control panel. ''Course, Maud, you prefer subtle light, don't you?'

Maud, spectacularly failing to cotton on, looked at her friend, confused. Perhaps all this was finally too much for her calm, collected pal. 'Oh no, I like to see what I'm up to...'

Myrtle nudged Maud and pointed to the main light switch.

And Maud cottoned on. 'Now you mention it,' she said, edging towards her goal, 'it's a bit harsh; shows up all my crow's feet and smile furrows.' She lunged at the switch and threw it.

The entire area was plunged into a weird, purple half-light.

Myrtle grabbed Maud. 'Quick! Run!' And with that they darted out of the main hatch.

The robots exchanged a deadpan look and then, in unison, strode off after the two humans. Haste was unnecessary - the targets' bio-metric parameters had been fully logged. Nothing would prevent the robots locating and eliminating their targets.

Unit Two, however, couldn't resist an 'Oy! come back!' Followed by a blast from its futuristic gun, which zapped into the tunnel wall showering the retreating figures with orange sparks.

Myrtle and Maud scurried down the tunnel heading for the secret passage, amazed that they'd been able to run further than the short distance to their bus stop without collapsing. However, they were struggling with the uneven ground and their forty-a-day habit.

'Oh, I'm getting all hot and bothered,' gasped Maud.

'Just... keep... going!' Myrtle could feel her lungs burning, her muscles seizing, and she didn't even want to think about what her varicose veins were up to.

'It's very strange; my Herbie has to wait a couple of weeks to see his bank manager, and now we're being chased by two of the blighters!' gasped Maud between laboured breaths, finally admitting defeat and stopping.

Myrtle stopped and looked round desperately. 'Quick! Down here!' She pointed to an alcove just up ahead. She threw herself into its dark recesses and slammed straight into something hard and unyielding, the impact of which propelled her backwards into the arms of Maud.

'It's a door!' hissed Maud to her dazed friend. She pushed past Myrtle and yanked it open. 'In!' She bundled Myrtle through the door, pulled it shut, put an arm around her pal and they both staggered into the dark.

'That's far enough,' said Maud, coming to a halt. 'Are you alright, love?'

Myrtle propped herself up against the damp brick wall of the passage. 'Never been better,' she gasped.

Maud took out the torch from her pocket and shone its dim beam down the passageway. 'Let's take a quick breather,' she suggested.

Myrtle nodded. 'Maybe we could surprise Her Majesty,' she quipped, peering into the gloom. Then a look of horror spread across her face. 'We've got to go back to that Nissen hut!'

'Are you out of your mind?! What about those robots?!'

'I reckon we've given them the slip, and I've got a nasty suspicion that those giant cheese plants are going to overrun the country,' she informed Maud. 'If not the whole planet.'

'Well, I hope they don't make a mess.'

'I doubt we'll be around to find out if we don't stop them,' responded Myrtle, totally missing Maud's gallows humour.

Maud looked even more flustered as she realised that Myrtle was serious. What on earth could they do about a load of rampaging plants? 'But, Myrtle, I can't even remember which button I pressed to start it all.'

'There must be something we can do?'

'We could go and get Roger,' suggested Maud.

Myrtle shot her a look of disbelief.

'The fire brigade, the police, the army…'

'Maud,' said Myrtle sternly, 'it would take too long. You saw how quickly those plants were spreading.'

'Ohh…' muttered Maud, beginning to feel the benefit of her earlier barley sugar wearing off.

Myrtle grabbed her by the shoulders. 'We caused this; we've got to stop it.'

'How about I sing to them?'

Myrtle shook her head. 'I know you can empty a pub with a few lines of "Knees Up Mother Brown", but those plants would strangle you before you had the chance.'

'Oh dear! How about I do it from a distance and sing loudly,' said Maud, her suggestions getting more ludicrous as her blood pressure soared.

'Wait a minute!' exclaimed Myrtle. 'The watering system!' Her eyes gleamed as a solution formulated in her mind. 'Maybe we could poison them.'

'Aye but what with? We left all our cleaning stuff on the platform,' Maud reminded her.

Myrtle looked downcast and slumped back against the wall.

It was Maud's turn to get all overexcited. 'Here, I've got my emergency bottle,' she said, pulling a small bottle out of her pocket. 'Mind, the emergency's usually a blocked drain, but it might work.' She passed the bottle to Myrtle, who vainly tried to read the annoyingly small print on the label.

'You'll have to read it, love; I've left my specs in the 1960s.'

Maud peered at the information. 'Hmm, lots of Buty- and Methyl-somethings and err…Benzy-something.'

26

'I reckon we're in with a chance.'

The two robot guardians, having followed the nano-DNA trail left by the two subjects on their way to the cryogenic stasis chamber, stepped through the entrance to the top-top secret base into the crumbling remains of the top secret base just as a tube train rattled through the disused station. Ignoring the flurry of nano-DNA whipped up by the airflow created by the primitive mode of transport favoured by so many of the local population, they paused, scanning for further traces of the subjects' nano-DNA.

'Residual DNA of the two targets verified. This galvanised steel receptacle belongs to one of the subjects designated for elimination and this ligneous implement with a coarse cellulose attachment belongs to the other subject. Conclusion: they have not exited in this direction,' stated Unit One.

Unit Two looked well narked. 'They've given us the slip and made us look like a right couple of plonkers.'

Chapter 5.

The two cleaning ladies had made it back to the Nissen hut without encountering so much as a twig, let alone a frenzied tidal wave of vegetation, which is what they'd half-expected. The plants were squished up against the portholes which lined the front section of the hut; apparently they had expanded into the entire structure.

There was no time to lose.

Myrtle instructed Maud to follow the pipe that ran along the front of the hut and find any kind of stopcock or control box. She sought out somewhere to put the emergency cleaning fluid into the watering system. She followed the pipe to the edge of the hut and squeezed into the gap between the hut and the far tunnel wall. She switched on Roger's torch; in the flickering light she could just see the pipe disappearing into the dark. Then she saw what she was looking for - a small tank feeding into the pipe. 'Any luck with the stopcock, Maud?' she called.

'Well, there's a big lever on the pipe just to the left of the stairs.'

'Is it open or closed?'

'It's in the closed position.'

'Good, stand by to open it when I say.' Myrtle edged her way to the tank and used the torch to prise the lid off.

Maud was dutifully standing-by at the bottom of the stairs to the main hatch, when she heard a soft, musical humming coming from the hut. It sounded like the tune she'd been humming earlier. Intrigued, she headed up the stairs. She reached the top; the calm, helpful voice announced that the re-animation process was entering its final stages. 'I don't think we've got much time, Myrtle,' she yelled.

Myrtle pulled out the bottle of toxic fluid, gave it a quick shake and opened it. 'Lord, what a pong!' she exclaimed. 'This duff must be steadly,' she concluded, as the pungent aroma floated up her nasal passages, sending disruptive signals to her cognitive processes. She poured the entire contents of the bottle into the tank. 'Alright, Sid, I mean, Saud, I mean, Maud,' she called, and started to make her way back.

Maud was edging towards one of the portholes, mesmerised by the plants which were swaying from side to side in time with the unearthly humming.

Myrtle reached the front corner of the hut and spotted Maud. 'Don't go weir that nindow!' she yelled.

At that moment the re-animation process was completed and all hell broke loose. With a tremendous screech the plants smashed through the porthole and entwined themselves round a rather surprised-looking Maud. 'Argh! Flippin' heck!!' she cried, trying to yank the giant cheese plants off her. 'HELP! MYRTLE!!'

With amazing speed the plants entwined themselves around Myrtle and dragged her towards the bottom of the stairs. 'Argh! Flippin' Nora,' exclaimed Myrtle.

'Myrtle,' beseeched Maud, the lack of oxygen making her head spin and Persian carpets materialise in front of her eyes.

The sound of her friend's desperate pleas gave Myrtle renewed energy and she lunged towards the lever. She managed to grab it but it would…not…budge. 'Come on, you pesky, ruddy thing!' she squawked. She felt it start to move and pulled. 'Cross your fingers, love,' she called to Maud, who had disconcertedly disappeared under layers of quivering foliage.

There was a terrible screech and the plants began shaking. Their grip loosened. Myrtle pulled them off herself and watched, transfixed, as they turned to wizened, yellow parchments. Rushing over to where she had last seen Maud she delved into the pile of dead leaves, which disintegrated and turned into dried flakes. She heard Maud spluttering.

'It worked,' croaked a surprised Maud.

A piercing alarm sounded from within the Nissen hut and the voice announced, 'Termination of sentient life forms verified.'

Myrtle helped Maud to her feet.

'Run?' asked Maud.

A look of concern spread across Myrtle's face as the disembodied voice intoned, 'Initiating obliteration protocols. This nuclear reactor is overloading.'

Myrtle grabbed Maud, who was in the process of making a speedy exit – a badly lit underground tunnel full of dead, alien plants wasn't really her scene.

'Wait up, Maud, I've got a nasty feeling Mayfair's about to be blown sky-high.' Myrtle dashed up the stairs and through the main hatch with a reluctant Maud in tow.

'Devastation radius confirmed as ten miles,' the voice informed them.

Myrtle rushed over to the main instrumentation banks and squinted at the readout panels, wishing she hadn't left her blessed specs in the 1960s. Her eyes widened as she reached the right distance to make sense of the diagram on the screen. 'Or more like half of London,' she said, with a sharp intake of breath.

'Flippin' heck, we're making a right hash of this,' said Maud, neatly summing up their handling of the ever-escalating predicament they'd blundered into. 'What are we going to do?'

Myrtle, who was darting between instrument panels giving the distinct impression of a demented woodpecker, stopped abruptly and directed her gaze towards Maud. 'We've got to shut it down…' she returned her attention to what looked like the main control panel and shook her head '…somehow.'

'I don't want to state the bloomin' obvious but, as you said earlier, it's a nuclear reactor not a washing machine.' She was fairly sure that you couldn't just turn it off by flicking a switch.

'This nuclear reactor is overloading,' the voice reminded them.

Myrtle looked intently at her friend. 'Maud, you know what I said about not pressing buttons?'

'Aye, I will never press another button ever again.'

'Well, ignore me! Start pressing!' she commanded, waving her hand toward the vast array of buttons available for such an activity.

Maud didn't need any further encouragement and joined Myrtle as they frantically pressed buttons and, for good measure, flicked switches at random.

The gradual buildup of power was now accelerating and the whining and rumbling increased. The two cleaning ladies could feel the floor vibrating and Maud noticed that a needle registering power levels had moved out of the green zone and into the orange zone.

'It's not working,' shrieked Maud, beginning to panic.

Myrtle, resisting the urge to break into a rousing chorus of "The White Cliffs of Dover", shouted, 'Keep calm, Maud. Where's your Dunkirk Spirit?'

'I left it in the 1960s!'

'This nuclear reactor is overloading.'

'We know, you stupid machine!' Maud was getting well and truly annoyed.

A bubble of inspiration popped in Myrtle's mind. 'Hold up! We could try blowing on it!'

'Blowing on it?!' exclaimed Maud - beyond annoyed, in fact nearing her wits' end.

'Aye, my Sid swears by it when he can't get the television set to warm up,' she explained. 'Come on, love, blow!' She took a deep breath and blew at the panel in front of her.

Large amounts of dust combined with dried flakes of dead alien plants flew into the air, irritating Maud's delicate nasal passages. She sneezed. Resigning herself to the escalating madness she followed Myrtle's lead. 'If you'd told me this morning…' deep breath, blow, 'we were going to end up…' deep breath, blow, 'blowing on a nuclear reactor to stop it from blowing up; no pun intended…' deep breath, blow, 'I'd have lost the will to… …' extra-deep breath followed by an extra-long blow, '…live!'

The plumes of dust shrouded Myrtle and Maud, who were hunched over the control panels, blowing, sneezing, and generally creating an eerie spectacle through the red glow that now infused the gallery.

The racket intensified and the entire hut shook right down to its foundations, making Myrtle and Maud's teeth clatter.

'This nuclear reactor is overloading,' the annoying voice calmly reminded them, counterpointing the mayhem exquisitely.

Myrtle cried out, 'It's not working!'

'Heck!' shouted Maud, pulling out her duster and mopping her glistening brow.

Myrtle stared at Maud, who looked as if she was about to have kittens. 'No! Wait, that's it! We've got to do the opposite!!'

'What?!' yelled Maud, who was now panicking for England - she could see the power readout needle teetering on the red zone.

'Start dusting!'

Myrtle and Maud frantically dusted some of the other banks of machines.

Maud wasn't at all sure what her friend intended to do; perhaps she was hoping that this would take their minds off the fact that they, along with a large chunk of London, were about to be blown to smithereens.

'Right, that should be enough,' shouted Myrtle. 'Start flapping!'

'I am flapping,' shrieked Maud who, in her opinion, had been doing her best impression of a headless chicken for most of their visit to the 1980s.

'No, the duster!' Myrtle shouted, dragging Maud over to the nuclear reactor. 'Into the reactor, quick!!'

They desperately flapped their dusters at the reactor, which continued its relentless crescendo.

Myrtle and Maud stepped back, closed their eyes and braced themselves.

'This nuclear reactor is...detecting foreign particles in the omnitronic relay circuits.' A harsh grinding noise joined the cacophony of sounds.

Myrtle and Maud stood frozen to the spot, not daring to breathe (a human's instinctive reaction to imminent death - after all if you're not breathing, you can't breathe your last! Obviously, a flawed assumption).

'This nuclear reactor is...shutting down.' The power buildup stopped and the racket subsided as the red light faded, replaced by the soft golden light.

Myrtle and Maud opened their eyes.

'Yes!' exclaimed a jubilant Myrtle.

'Aye!' agreed an ecstatic Maud.

'Let's get out of here before something else happens.'

They turned to leave and there, blocking their path, were the robots, who stood scanning and processing the multitude of data that threatened to overload their sub-processors, median-processors and primary-processors.

Finally, Unit One cut to the chase. 'You have destroyed the life forms,' it stated.

Myrtle drew herself up to her full height of five-foot-not-very-much. 'Aye, we're not as harmless as we look.'

Unit One's sub-routines went back into overdrive as it computed the inescapable fact that its primary mission a) had failed, and b) was over.

Unit Two lurked in the background, shuffling the remains of their primary mission around the floor with its foot.

'If you're here to have a chat about my Herbie's overdraft, you're over twenty years too late!' said Maud. She turned to Myrtle and yelled, 'Sebastian Coe!'

Myrtle frowned. 'What?'

'I mean let's go!'

And with that the ladies slipped past the robots and were gone.

Unit One stared after them, calculating its next move. Activating shutdown protocols seemed high on its to-do list.

Unit Two had a much better idea. 'Get 'em,' it growled and shot off.

Unit One faltered. Then its mutual support system overrode its shutdown protocols, and it gave chase.

Myrtle and Maud scampered up the tunnel, making it to the secret passage in double-quick time. They knew there was no chance of outwitting the robots on this occasion, they had to make it to street level. The sound of Unit Two ranting and raving behind them spurred them on. They dashed headlong towards the glimmer of light they could see at the end of the passage.

Sensing that Maud was flagging, Myrtle gave her an encouraging, 'We're nearly there, love.'

They shot through the heavy metal door and collided with a small group of startled people. 'Mind ourselves,' shouted Myrtle. She heaved the door shut and, with Maud's help, slid the bolts back into place. They both leant their backs against the door and caught their breath, confident that the door posed a sufficient barrier to delay their pursuers. But the robots had other ideas, and bricks and mortar rained down on the ladies as the robots started to demolish the walls on either side of the door. 'Persistent blighters aren't they,' remarked Myrtle, as they dashed off past the line of gobsmacked people.

Much to the amazement of the group of people, two men covered in dust, who looked rather like 1960s bank managers, emerged from the holes and stormed past them. Astonished, they watched them go by and head up the corridor.

After a short pause a bearded man dressed in a long, sheepskin coat spoke up. 'Err, I think Roger was right - the Strand station would be better.'

This was met with general agreement amongst the group, along the lines of:

'Yah.'

'Okay.'

'Can do.'

Chapter 6.

The sight of two dishevelled cleaning ladies tumbling out onto the street raised a few eyebrows amongst the smart passers-by, but no more than that.

Maud clung onto the nearest lamp post - she was keen to collapse in a heap, but she didn't want to let the side down.

Myrtle could feel her varicose veins throbbing and her knees beginning to buckle but, like Maud, she'd been brought up never to make an exhibition of herself, especially in a public place. Lying around gasping for breath on a street in Mayfair was definitely not on, so she joined Maud and clung onto the lamp post.

Between gulps of air Maud managed to say, 'We've got to find Rog…er. Where the heck is…that posh boozer?'

'No time for that. You've got…the keys,' gasped Myrtle, staggering the mercifully short distance to the minibus. 'Jump in and drive.'

'Oh, aye.'

They clambered into the vehicle. The tired engine shuddered into life, and with an excruciating crunch of gears the minibus juddered up the street.

The robots emerged from the station's entrance. Scanning the street, they homed in on the two figures in the departing minibus, confirming their targets.

'We must appropriate a motorised vehicle,' stated Unit One, smashing the driver's window of a parked car.

This action raised more than a few eyebrows amongst the smart passers-by. In fact, a city gent, dressed in similar but dust-free attire, strode purposefully over to remonstrate with them; only to have a sudden change of heart when Unit Two scowled at him.

Unit Two got into the passenger seat. Unit One glared at the dashboard, the engine roared into life, and with a lot of acceleration the tyres squealed and the car shot off, leaving a layer of black rubber on the street, and a crowd of shocked bystanders.

In the labouring minibus Maud continued to crunch her way through the gear box (or what was left of it), and plumes of acrid smoke billowed from the exhaust. 'Flippin' Nora!' she cried, glancing into the rearview mirror. 'They've pinched a car and they're catching us! Ohhh, they must be very cross.'

Myrtle craned her neck round to see for herself. 'I don't think robots are programmed to get cross.' Her eyes widened as the car surged forward and rammed the minibus, which lurched and shuddered throwing Myrtle and Maud forward.

Maud, struggling to control the minibus, said dryly, 'Do you want to tell them or shall I?'

'Just drive!'

Maud slammed the gear stick into third.

'Faster!' pleaded Myrtle.

'Why did you get me to drive? I'm getting in a right old tizzy.'

'You used to drive General Wheeler-Carmichael during the war, didn't you?'

'Aye, but that was a Rolls Royce and we were never chased by killer bank managers.'

'Try double de-clutching, love,' suggested Myrtle.

'Oh aye.' And by doing just that she coaxed the minibus up through the gears. 'That's more like it,' she said, relaxing slightly as they pulled away from their pursuers. 'I just hope I don't have to parallel park this beast.'

'Don't worry, love, I'll get out and wave my arms around in an unhelpful manner,' Myrtle said, with a smile.

Maud smiled. 'Ta, love. Ohh,' she announced, 'I'm getting one of them urges again!'

'What now?!'

'Well, besides wanting to give this dashboard a good old dust, I'm getting a really strong urge to buy those British Telecom shares again.'

'Well, control yourself...hang on! Now you mention it - I'm getting an urge to buy some British Gas shares. I must remember to tell Sid.'

'Ohh! And now I'm desperate to have an outrageously large hairstyle. Do you think it would be a good look on me?' she asked, removing her headscarf and giving her hair a shake.

Myrtle looked at her friend. 'Well, it might,' she said, thinking anything would be an improvement to the flat, lanky locks that were invariably hidden by one of Maud's colourful headscarves. Not that she could talk.

'Let's find out,' said Maud. She screeched to a halt outside a conveniently-placed hairdressers.

Whilst they were fumbling around trying to work out how the heck to open the doors, a thought struck Myrtle. 'Wait up, how are we going to pay? I've only got tuppence on me.'

'We could rob a bank,' suggested Maud.

'Rob a bank!' exclaimed Myrtle. 'The 1980s is having a very peculiar effect on you, I must say.'

Maud looked contrite and said, 'Don't worry, I've got my bob-a-job purse with me.'

Moments later the robots' car came careering up the high street. Spotting the abandoned minibus, they pulled over. Logic stated that their targets were attempting to escape on foot; it did not even occur to the robots that they might have gone for a shampoo and set. So they started searching the high street and market area using their body recognition software.

Sometime later two ladies with bouffant hair emerged from the hairdressers and made a beeline for the nearby department store.

The robots, having failed to locate their targets in the surrounding area, returned to the corner of the high street just as the two ladies disappeared into the store.

A while later the 'bouffant hair' ladies came out of the store wearing garish, floral-print skirts, flouncy blouses, and jackets with shoulder pads that would put an American footballer to shame. To say that they had the 'POW factor' would be an understatement. They exited the store with such exquisite deportment that, if they'd been so inclined, they could have processed up the grand staircase of Buckingham Palace, executed a deep court curtsey and retreated; all with Debrett's Peerage balanced on their heads. So, it was no great surprise that it was only when they got into the minibus and drove off that the robots realised that they were their targets. The robots dashed across the road, leapt into their car and sped off in hot pursuit.

Maud was once more at the wheel and Myrtle was extolling the virtues of her 1980's makeover. 'Whoever thought up power dressing was a genius and no doubt.'

Maud nodded and adjusted the rearview mirror so she could apply her free gift lipstick - a glorious shade of shocking pink. 'I tell you what, those bank managers are rather dishy, aren't they?'

Myrtle, who was back-combing her hair for maximum effect, paused briefly to consider Maud's statement. 'Come to think of it, you're right.' Returning to her hair she started plastering it with maximum-hold hairspray: her free gift. Hairdressers in the 1980s were very generous, she had to say, looking forward to trying out her maximum-hold hair gel later. ''Course robots don't,' she said, glancing up at their route. 'Oh, take the next left.'

'Don't what?' enquired Maud, manoeuvring the minibus round the tight left-hand turn with ease. She was really getting the hang of this minibus driving lark and was beginning to wonder if she might try something even bigger when she got back to the 1960s.

'Well, as far as I can tell from the television, they don't do it.'

'Don't do what?'

'You know. What you and your Herbie do of a Saturday night.'

'What, the washing up?' said Maud, puzzled.

'No! It!!' said Myrtle insistently. 'You know…'

'You're going to have to spell it out for me, love.'

'S-E-X!'

'Oh,' said a disappointed Maud. She screeched to a halt; with her romantic notions shattered, for some reason she needed to go shopping. 'Look, there's another department store.'

'But we've already got our gorgeous outfits.'

'I want to get my Herbie some presents from the 1980s,' said Maud, feeling guilty about having carnal thoughts about someone other than her husband.

Myrtle, who rarely had carnal thoughts of any nature, even about her husband, said, 'We haven't got time for that.'

But Maud was already reeling off her shopping list. 'An electronic calculator, a digital watch, a Filofax - whatever that lot is, and a pair of red braces.'

Suddenly there was a loud bang and the minibus shuddered as a bright orange beam of light made a hole the size of a bucket in the back doors. Myrtle glanced in the wing mirror and through the mist she saw the robots' car in the far distance speeding towards them. 'For goodness sake, Maud, get us out of here!'

'Alright, no need to get all bitchy.'

'God dammit, Maud!' responded an exasperated Myrtle.

'Language!'

Myrtle turned to Maud and glared at her. 'My hair is bigger than yours,' she declared.

'Well, my shoulder pads are bigger than yours,' riposted Maud, arching an eyebrow.

Myrtle felt a strange urge to grab Maud by her shoulder pads and shake her, but contented herself with, 'My husband's oil company is bigger and better than yours, I'll have you know.'

ZAP! Another energy bolt seared through the back door, turning the hole the size of a bucket into a hole the size of a much larger bucket, jolting the two pals back to reality.

'What are you on about?!' asked Maud.

Myrtle shrugged her extra-big shoulders. 'No idea. Blimey, I think we'd better get back to the 1960s P.D.Q.'

Fortunately, the Thurrock factory was having an uneventful morning. No problems with the production line or the newly installed office computer system, and no lorries turning up with shirty drivers at the wheel desperate to 'job and knock': a time honoured ploy prevalent in the haulage industry, and many others, allowing both the employer and employee to labour under the mutual illusion that they are both getting one over on the other and therefore winning. Independent adjudicators are still considering this one, but it's safe to say that, as with most things in the Multiverse, victories are fleeting, as are the extra hours gained from knocking off work early.

The side annex to the Thurrock warehouse was quiet when Myrtle and Maud came rushing in. Myrtle proceeded to pace up and down whilst Maud kept a nervous eye on the door, which they hadn't even bothered to shut, lock, or barricade due to the robots' disregard for the polite use of specifically designed entrances to buildings.

'I've got to think what my Sid would do and then do the opposite,' said Myrtle.

Maud looked sceptical.

'Well, it worked with the nuclear reactor,' Myrtle reminded her.

Maud nodded.

'I know, we've got to retrace our steps. Sid says, "Never go back if you can go forward." Mind, that's when he used to play football, but it might work.'

Maud could feel her blood pressure rising. 'We've got to get back to the 1960s,' she squawked, 'but how?!'

Coming to an abrupt halt, Myrtle swung round. 'It's them groovy mats!' she cried. 'They're the only things that hadn't changed when we first got here.'

'So?'

'So, they must have come with us.'

'What good's a couple of mats?' asked a bemused Maud. 'S'pose they might cushion our fall when they kill us. That would be nice,' she said sardonically.

At that moment the two robots came storming through the door and levelled their guns at the ladies.

Maud closed her eyes and waited for the inevitable, wondering what a beam of light which could make a sizeable hole in metal would do to her ample proportions. 'Hang on a mo' lads,' she heard Myrtle say. 'Actually, we'd quite like to hear your life story before we pop our clogs, wouldn't we, Maud?'

Maud's eyes shot open. 'Aye, you've obviously had an interesting life, what with coming from another planet and such like.'

'You've changed your tune,' said Unit Two.

'Well, that was earlier. Go on son, get it all off your chest,' said Myrtle.

Unit One, in full control of its logic centres, said, 'Registering human deception.'

'No, they understand how lonely we are.'

'You require a diagnostic of your personality routines.'

Unit Two ignored it and addressed the cleaning ladies, who had taken the opportunity to edge towards the mats and were almost there. 'I'll just reset my I.Q. so I can tell you the full low-down.'

'Alright, love,' said Myrtle. She took two tissues out of her pocket, passed one to Maud, tore hers in half and stuffed them in her ears.

With a wink Maud did the same.

'This bi-pedal, adaptive unit was activated on Universal Temporal Code 00.002002.2033,' it began, looking all po-faced again. 'Adaptive personality download completed on UTC 00.00200…'

Myrtle and Maud took a step sideways, felt the soft cushion of the mats under their feet, exchanged a hopeful glance and crossed their fingers. In an instant they were both engulfed by two funnels of swirling, blue light and vanished before the robots' visual input devices.

Without all the "ohhing" and "ahhing" of their inaugural time travel journey, Myrtle and Maud were able to register the experience more fully.

Myrtle, for some strange reason, started thinking about her shopping list for the week ahead, and had got as far as one pound of sugar and half a pound of butter when the tumultuous clamour of shadows overwhelmed her: whether or not shadows could tumultuously clamour was another thing all together, but that's how it felt to Myrtle.

Maud's experience was much calmer: she didn't think about anything as she floated towards the distant murmur of memories coalescing into a beautiful melody.

They did both experience the temporal boom again, although happily its deafening effects were lessened by the large amount of tissue paper that the ladies had thrust into their ears.

At the PLOTLINE monitoring station Myrtle and Maud's widely anticipated incursion back into the Wave of Temporalati activated the system, which had been hanging around on standby.

'Alert,' intoned the soothing voice, as the alarm sounded. 'PLOTLINE monitoring system activated. Time travel confirmed. Origin: the 11th October 1987. Destination: the 11th October 1965. Categorised as level one incursion.' The alarm changed key and intensified. 'PLOTLINE intervention critical.' The insistent alarm continued and ACTION flashed up on the banks of screens.

Chapter 7.

Fortunately, the Thurrock factory circa 1965 was also having an uneventful morning. This is the Multiverse's *de rigueur* way of intuitively harmonising the fine balance of events. In this case, if anyone had been in the warehouse to witness the departure of Myrtle and Maud via two funnels of swirling, blue light and the instantaneous return of two immaculately coiffured, power dressed women who bore a passing resemblance to the two dowdy ladies who were always on hand to offer a kindly ear over a cuppa, there would have been pandemonium and the entire workforce would have knocked off early, causing all kinds of ripples in the Wave of Temporalati, from the shirty truck drivers unable to load their lorries, to the customers unable to buy their usual shade of light blue stationary, thus delaying vital correspondence with potentially catastrophic results.

So next time you're having a dull, boring, and mundane day remember that somewhere, someone is having totally bizarre day which you really don't want to know about.

At a pinch, 'totally bizarre' would sum up the kind of day Myrtle and Maud were having.

After a few seconds acclimatising to being back on *terra firma*, which involved swaying around with a startled look on their faces, waiting for the ringing in their ears to stop, Myrtle and Maud stepped off the mats and gazed around at their surroundings.

'Well, everything looks nice and 1960s,' said Myrtle, as they both extracted the pieces of tissue from their ears.

'Aye.'

'You look ridiculous,' blurted out Myrtle, her social filters crumbling in her disorientated state.

'So do you.' Maud frowned. 'I don't think I'm going to like the 1980s.'

Myrtle's eyes darted from side to side and she tugged at her hair.

Maud smiled, chuckled and then broke into a belly laugh as only someone who had travelled in time, saved the planet along with half of London, and avoided death a couple of times could laugh. And it wasn't long before Myrtle joined in and the two friends were waving their arms around helplessly, gasping for breath and wiping away the tears streaming down their faces.

The hilarity of their situation gradually subsided and the reassuring sound of the kettle boiling diverted the ladies away from the uncontrollable giggles that kept threatening to re-emerge; which was a good job because their ribs were aching.

Myrtle spotted her tobacco tin resting on the table where she'd left it. She grabbed it, opened it and inhaled the aroma. 'Bliss!'

Maud pottered over and switched the kettle off at the wall socket. 'Cuppa, Myrtle?' asked Maud, oblivious to the fact that the time machine was powering down.

'Oh, ta, love,' said Myrtle, flopping down into the chair and proceeding to roll a ciggie. She distractedly watched Maud as she ambled around warming up the pot and babbling away about giving up reading tea leaves. 'You know, I reckon we should stop this cleaning malarky.'

Maud was counting out the number of teaspoons of tea leaves under her breath. 'Three, four, and one for the pot.' She poured the boiling water into the pot and gave the brew a vigorous stir. 'Why?' she asked, putting the tea cosy onto the pot. 'Because it gets us into right pickles?'

Myrtle smiled. 'No, I was thinking how your emergency fluid killed all those plants.'

'So?' Maud reached through the small window to grab the milk bottle which was keeping coolish on the window sill and gave it a quick sniff.

Myrtle was carefully flexing her feet in a vain attempt to relax her calf muscles, which were beginning to seize up. 'Well, we use them every day…'

Maud looked across at her in surprise.

'Alright, every other day.'

Another look from Maud.

'Once a week, then.'

'Aye, but we're not giant cheese plants, are we? It would probably take thirty years to affect us and we'll be dead by then,' Maud said blithely, picking up the tray and carrying it over. She placed it on the table and poured two cups. 'Oh, no!'

'What?!'

'In all the excitement I've only just remembered - I left my lucky mop on that platform. Blast! That's twenty-two years bad luck, knowing my luck,' she concluded, passing Myrtle her cuppa.

'Ta, love.' Myrtle settled back in her chair, blew softly at the steaming liquid and took a sip. 'Lovely!' Another sip. 'It was your lucky mop that got us into this, er... that.'

Maud plonked herself down onto a chair, slipped off her comfortable shoes, wiggled her toes, and looked longingly at her cuppa - she always marvelled at Myrtle's asbestos gullet which enabled her to drink boiling hot tea. 'Aye, and my strange fascination with buttons.'

'Don't talk to me about buttons,' said Myrtle, who proceeded to drain her cup. 'Hang on! What about the twin-tub, er, time machine?' She looked round and there was the offending machine innocently sitting in the corner. 'Heck, this time travelling lark is very confusing.'

'Is it?' said Maud. Unable to wait any longer, she picked up her tea cup, poured a small amount into her saucer and slurped it down - not the most elegant way to drink a cuppa, but a time honoured way of cooling it down. Well, that was her excuse. She sighed. 'That's a lovely cuppa. Isn't it strange how sometimes tea really hits the spot?'

'Hmm,' replied Myrtle, only half-listening. 'I'm just thinking; we definitely didn't see the time machine in the 1980s, did we?'

'No.'

'That's alright then. For one terrible moment I thought those robots might be able to follow us.'

'Why don't you have a top-up?' said Maud, reaching over to pour Myrtle another cuppa, but Myrtle was staring in the direction of the time machine. 'Myrtle? Yoo-hoo!'

Myrtle eased herself to her feet. 'I just heard a weird beeping noise.'

'Must be an after effect of that loud boom we heard when we were whooshing through time.'

'No, there it is again.'

Maud slipped her comfy shoes back on and went to join Myrtle, who was standing a few feet away from the time machine. 'I can't hear anything,' she said. 'It's not your tinnitus flaring up again?' She cautiously approached the time machine and give it a light tap with her knuckles. 'You see, dead as a doornail, love.'

At that moment the small door to the warehouse creaked open, the ladies whirred round and three people - well, they looked like people to Myrtle and Maud, but who can tell these days - stepped into the warehouse. They were each dressed in a grey, functional uniform which, in comparison to the bold, bright outfits that Myrtle and Maud were wearing, looked dull and nondescript. Myrtle noticed that they were each wearing a chunky belt with pouches attached; she assumed that the contents of these must be the tools of their trade - obviously a bucket didn't quite cut it in their line of business.

The weird beeping sound that Myrtle had heard was coming from a handheld device that one of the new arrivals was pointing in their direction. 'Confirmed,' said the young woman.

The serious, older-looking woman, who had obviously been waiting for something to be confirmed, stepped forward and smiled. 'Good morning,' she said, her dulcet tones inspiring potentially misplaced confidence in her good intentions.

'Morning,' said Maud, going to shake the women's hand. 'I'm Maud and this is Myrtle.'

The woman's demeanour remained calm and composed as she returned the introductions. 'I'm Roz and this is Hadron.'

The young woman glanced up from the fascinating device. 'Hi.'

'And this is Syntax.'

The young man stepped forward and grinned at them. 'Awesome!' Myrtle's expression remained impassive.

'We're from the PLOTLINE agency,' Roz informed them.

'What's that?' asked a wary Myrtle.

'Protecting the Legitimate, Official Timeline agency,' clarified Hadron.

'Eh?'

'We keep an eye on time travellers,' explained Syntax, who was looking around the drab interior of the warehouse like a kid in a sweet shop.

Myrtle's guard dropped slightly, although she noticed that the group were still blocking the route to the main exit.

Roz, a seasoned PLOTLINE operative, sensed Myrtle's mistrust and moved further into the warehouse, glancing around as if she was wandering round a museum. She paused by the time machine satisfying herself that it was non-operational and then directed an inquiring look at the two ladies. 'Time travel, ladies?'

'Well, we've certainly done some of that today,' said Myrtle, seeing no reason to keep quiet about it. After all, they all seemed nice and polite, and they weren't trying to garrotte them, blast holes in them, or generally eliminate them.

'Would you like a cuppa?' asked Maud. 'There's plenty in the pot.'

Roz smiled. 'Thank you.'

'Help me get the cups, Myrtle,' said Maud, heading off towards the tea-making area, hoping that there would be enough clean cups. 'How do you lot take it?' she called over her shoulder.

'As it comes, thanks,' replied Roz. Beckoning her two subordinates over, she waited for the ladies to be out of earshot. 'Right,' she glanced over at the ladies who appeared to be doing some washing up, 'as we've only registered a slight distortion in the timeline, we just need to make sure that there isn't going to be a delayed timeline reaction. Hadron, how long do you think we'll need for the D.T.R scan?'

'About five minutes, give or take.'

'OK, let's get them to give us a quick rundown of their movements in the…?' she looked at Hadron, who studied her device - technically a temporal utility device.

'1980s, Roz. 1987 to be exact.'

'Right. Syntax, I think this would be a perfect opportunity to put your training into practice.'

'Cool, thanks, Roz,' an eager Syntax replied.

Myrtle and Maud returned with three cups and saucers. 'Strong and sweet I think is the order of the day,' said Maud, pouring the somewhat stewed tea into the waiting cups. Myrtle spooned generous amounts of sugar into the dark brown liquid.

'Thanks,' said Roz and Hadron.

Syntax took his cup and gulped down the high-grade liquid. 'Cheers,' he spluttered, then took out his temporal utility device from his belt. 'So, tell me about your time travels.'

Myrtle didn't beat around the bush. 'Well, you probably won't believe it, but we've just been to the 1980s.'

'Oh, yes…' began Syntax, hoping to get a little more information out of the ladies and thereby impress Roz. He had to find a way of keeping them talking.

He didn't need to worry as Maud joined in. 'Aye, we had a right old time of it, didn't we, Myrtle?'

'A right old time,' she agreed.

'First, we met this ok-yah chap who thought we looked like Harold Wilson. I ask you…!'

Roz, who could see a long-winded story a light-year away, tapped Hadron on the arm and indicated that they should leave Syntax to it.

'He convinced us to do this cleaning job up in town…' Maud was in full flow.

From a safe distance, Roz watched Syntax with a faint smile on her face. She leant over to Hadron and whispered into her ear. 'I think you could take this opportunity to check the temporal regulators.' A task that required plenty of time.

Hadron nodded. Although not an old-timer like Roz, she too could spot a drama-saga at ten paces. She sidled over to the rather nifty black phone sitting on one of the filing cabinets.

'…The traffic was terrible! I've never seen so many cars in all my days. It was like Piccadilly Circus.'

'Hmm, Maud. That's because it **was** Piccadilly Circus, love.'

'Was it? Oh…well, anyway, then…'

Hadron reached the location of the phone (more correctly categorised as a fixed point, vocal receiver-transmitter device with a slow-dial feature), picked up the receiver and dialled, slowly.

There was a crackle as the line connected and the melodious voice spoke to Hadron. 'At the third stroke the time will be seven fifty-five and twenty seconds.' Pip, pip, pipppp. Hadron studied her temporal utility device checking that the local time matched the PLOTLINE agency's central time.

By now Myrtle had managed to get back in on the act. '...Underground station. Don't tell a soul, but I worked there during the war, you see, and I wanted to show Maud...'

'At the third stroke the time will be eight ten precisely,' Pip, pip, pipppp.

Maud was off again. 'I can't tell you how scary it was. There was a weird green glow...'

'At the third stroke the time will be eight twenty-two...'

Roz, unable to take anymore, strode over to Hadron, took the receiver from her and slammed it back into its cradle. 'Ladies,' she said in her most commanding voice, making Maud pause mid-sentence. 'I'm afraid we're on a bit of a tight schedule, if I may sum up your adventures?'

Maud looked crestfallen, but then she noticed the glazed look in even Syntax's eyes and realised she'd overdone it. 'By all means,' she said, thinking to herself that this woman would have to be damn smart to sum up the type of day they'd had.

'Would I be correct in saying... it's been the experience of a lifetime?'

'Aye, that's the long and short of it,' confirmed Maud, impressed.

'Excellent,' said Roz. 'Hadron, Syntax.' Her sharp tone jolted them back into professional mode. 'We can proceed with the memory erasure.'

'Memory erasure?' Myrtle wasn't sure if she liked the sound of that.

'Yeah, we need to wipe your memories of the time you spent in the 1980s,' explained Syntax, still looking haunted by the experience of trying to look remotely interested in the ladies' ramblings, but valiantly trying to hide it as he busied himself adjusting the settings on his temporal utility device.

'Oh, I see,' said Myrtle.

'We do understand,' said Roz, 'most people are reluctant to forget.'

'Oh, no. That's fine. I think I'd have terrible nightmares if you didn't.'

'You're not wrong, love,' Maud concurred. 'When I think of those dingy tunnels, deadly plants, killer bank managers...'

Myrtle could see Maud was in danger of getting into her stride again, so she cut her off with a curt, 'Maud!'

Hadron and Syntax pointed their devices at Myrtle and Maud, and a beam of crimson energy shot out, hitting the ladies' foreheads.

'Ohh…' they both muttered, their eyes widened and they slipped into a trance.

Hadron and Syntax deactivated the beams and Syntax proceeded to scan Myrtle and Maud.

'Memory erasure in progress. No abnormal reactions. Possible peripheral memory loss,' he reported, keen to impress Roz after his earlier unprofessional zoning-out.

Hadron replaced her device into her belt. 'Well, that was an interesting way to pass some time,' she remarked.

'Hmm, let's get out of here before they come to and start wittering on again,' said Roz.

The PLOTLINE operatives pressed a button on their temporal utility devices, the soles of their boots glowed bright blue and a pool of sparkling, blue energy fizzed around their boots.

'This location seems to be a bit of a time travel hotspot, doesn't it…?' Roz commented, her voice fading as the bright blue funnels of light swirled around them and they disappeared.

For Myrtle and Maud time passed in the only way time can pass when one is in a trance having one's memory engrams rearranged: S-L-O-W…oh, what's the word?

The annex to the Thurrock warehouse remained unusually quiet. Let's face it, the Multiverse is as infinitely wise as it is big.

Oh, yes…S-L-O-W-**L-Y**.

Maud blinked. 'Now, where was I?' she began, then on seeing Myrtle she exclaimed, 'What have you done to your hair?!'

Myrtle blinked.

'And what are you wearing?!'

Myrtle looked at her in astonishment. 'I could ask you the very same!'

There they stood gawping at each other until Myrtle took a deep breath and said, 'I think we need a cuppa and a ciggie, don't you?'

Maud gave her chum a thoughtful look, took a couple of paces backwards and started moving her outstretched arms in a circular motion.

'What are you doing, love?' asked a bemused Myrtle.

'Warming up!'

'Warming up?'

'Aye, I've got this strange urge to increase my aerobic capacity.'

'Your what?!' exclaimed a mystified Myrtle.

'Come on, love, give it a go!' encouraged Maud.

Myrtle watched her friend for a few seconds, glanced over at her tobacco tin, and then joined in.

At that precise moment the infinite wisdom of the Multiverse chose to pounce and the day shift arrived.

The remarkable sartorial transformation of the cleaning ladies, combined with the shock of seeing them standing, no… **exercising** in a smoke-free area, had an intoxicating effect on them and Myrtle and Maud's keep-fit class was an instant hit.

Chapter 8.

Clear evidence of the complex nature of one of the basic constituents of the Multiverse - lateral spacio-flux causality - can be seen at this point. In that, whilst Myrtle and Maud's keep-fit class was in full swing, a seemingly unrelated drama was unfolding deep within an alien underground base not far from the Thurrock factory.

A drama that could, nevertheless, put the newfound health kick of the Thurrock workers in jeopardy; not to mention the future of the Earth.

The origin of this potentially catastrophic *contretemps* can be traced back to three inconsequential events that happened an hour or so earlier: two serious-looking men setting up an observation point in the fields overlooking the factory, Myrtle and Maud being dropped off for work, and a peckish Molly and James leaving the warehouse.

The two dour, middle-aged men were dressed in a bizarre mixture of 1960s fashion: both wore an oxygenated-blood-red Guards tunic, the gold buttons of which strained to contain the rotund nature of their stomachs, and garish, florid flared trousers. This bizarre concoction of psychedelic attire could have just about been carried off by men half their age but, whilst providing the hi-vis requirements of their work, on these two it produced a disquieting sight indeed.

'Right, we need level and stable ground, Fred,' instructed Ron, whose short, greying hair and moustache made him look even more ridiculous in his way-out clothing.

The two men inspected the surrounding ground.

Fred at least had the advantage of a full head of blond hair, but he still looked way too way-out. He stomped around in his hybrid safety boots and on selecting a suitable area said, 'Level and stable, check.'

Delving into their flight cases, they each took out a pair of safety goggles - their primary function being to protect the wearer from various hazards; anything from the plasma glare of irradiated atmospheres to low-flying projectiles - and a pair of heavy-duty, polymeric gloves: designed to safeguard the wearer from a wide range of dangers, from handling plasmatic heat exchanges to squishing a finger in a slamming door. They put them on and then checked that each other's safety wear was optimally employed as recommended by their Induction manual known as the USELESS manual: the Universal Safety Executive's Legislation Enabling Statutory Safety.

They opened their terrain-adaptive chairs, did a final weight-bearing check and sat down. They pulled out their hi-tech binoculars. Designed to watch mission targets from a safe distance, their hi-tech features included real-time direct streaming, facial recognition, and risk assessment monitoring.

Fully prepared, they settled back to watch the primary observation target-zone: the Thurrock factory.

Minutes passed and nothing happened. Nothing related to their mission, that is. A couple of crows swooped in and perched on the dilapidated roof of the primary observation target-zone, and a milk-float jingled slowly up a nearby road.

With a frustrated sign Fred lowered his hi-tech binoculars. 'I can't believe how boring the 1960s are; I thought it was meant to be all groovy and happening.'

Ron, accustomed to Fred's short attention span, continued scanning the designated area and zoomed in on their secondary subject's motorised vehicle. 'I know we're dressed for Carnaby Street, but this is Surrey.'

'More's the pity.'

'Stop your moaning. You should know by now that these pre-emptive Health and Safety assessments are time consuming.'

Fred took out a gadget from his flight case, eased himself into a more comfortable position, and started reviewing the data they had already gathered. 'I think we're wasting our time. We've already witnessed Sara Wright's... the primary subject's,' Fred corrected himself before Ron had the chance, 'total disregard for Health and

Safety issues, and there's no way her grandmother will be any different.'

Exasperated, Ron lowered his hi-tech binoculars and addressed his long-time colleague directly. 'Look, we've got to get indisputable, retrospective proof that it's part of the primary subject's genetic make-up: the grandmother gene.'

'I know,' grumbled Fred.

'And judging by her motorised vehicle, I've got a suspicion that this particular grandmother is going to be an ideal subject,' he continued, his stern look disguising any pleasure he was deriving from this fact. 'But we don't want to risk missing out on our temporal trauma allowance twice in a row, now do we?'

'No,' said a horrified Fred, remembering how it took all of ten minutes to get the incontrovertible proof they needed on Sara Wright.

Ron returned to his observation of the primary target-zone. 'We don't want to lose our place at the top of the financially beneficial booking off league. I reckon we should aim for, hmm… let's say six hours and fifteen minutes.'

'Yeah, but what if she takes too long to reveal her high-risk DNA and we end up in temporal decompression?'

'Temporal decompression!' cried Ron in disgust. 'Don't get me wrong, I like rules and regulations as much as the next person, but spending time being assessed and treated for temporal trauma is the last thing I want to do after a long shift. You'd better set a thirty minute reminder alert to be on the safe side.'

'OK,' said Fred. Lifting up the sleeve of his tunic he shouted, 'Set alarm one,' at the chunky black gadget strapped to his wrist, which responded with a beep. 'Makes you wonder, though?'

'What?'

'Why the powers that be think temporal trauma is more likely after twelve hours?'

'It's true,' stated Ron. 'I've seen the graph. There's a 30-45% chance of temporal trauma after six hours; hence the allowance.'

'What, to keep us sweet?'

'Yes, and to cover themselves. After twelve hours there's a 95% chance of trauma; something to do with being out of sync with your personal time stream; can cause havoc apparently. Remember Filo and Tarn? They once spent thirteen hours in the 1970s and…wait.' He leant forward in anticipation. A small door housed in the large warehouse doors opened. 'There's movement in the specified zone.'

Fred reached for his hi-tech binoculars and zoomed in on the two figures emerging from the building.

The facial-recognition software built into both sets of binoculars zoned in and CONFIRMED flashed up on the screens.

'Right; secondary subject confirmed as Molly Wright, Mrs, and tertiary subject confirmed as James Harper, Mr. Looks like they're heading for the secondary subject's motorised vehicle,' intoned Ron, setting his binoculars to real-time streaming mode.

Anticipating a potential risk-related situation developing, Fred scanned the road leading up to the factory. 'Here, there's two old biddies heading towards Molly and James.'

'You mean two ancillary subjects are heading towards the secondary and tertiary subjects,' Ron corrected him.

'Yeah, whatever, they're not paying any attention to the road. I can see a delta plus risk-related road incident developing.'

Ron, still focusing on the secondary and tertiary subjects, said, 'Hang on, the secondary subject is opening the boot of her motorised vehicle and she's reaching for something. We might be edging into an epsilon plus risk-related incident,' he said. 'We can wave our trauma allowance goodbye if she's reaching for a jetpack,' he concluded dryly.

Molly Wright - secondary subject, grandmother of Sara Wright, secret agent and super-deluxe person; however you wish to describe her - was indeed reaching for something, but nothing as exciting or cutting edge as a jetpack. Her memory was a bit sketchy at present, but she knew she was feeling hungry. She pulled out a hamper and placed it on the bonnet of her car. 'Luckily, I packed a light supper,' she remarked, 'which, judging by the position of the sun, is going to be a light breakfast.' She paused, a look of consternation on her face. 'Now, how do I remember that?'

'You always pack a light supper when we go off investigating,' James reminded her.

'Do I?'

James nodded.

Molly opened the hamper and, on seeing the contents, she had a vivid flashback and could see herself putting the items into the hamper. She frowned. 'I've just remembered, I've got an eidetic memory.' She looked at James, baffled. 'How could I have forgotten that?'

'You're hungry, that's all,' he reassured her, peering into the hamper. 'Ah! Smoked salmon and champagne.'

Fred was still focusing on the ancillary subjects, who he assumed were professional cleaners, going by their attire and well-stocked buckets. They had reached Molly and James and were in conversation with them. He relaxed a little and reduced the potential risk-related scenario to alpha minus.

At that moment James directed his gaze towards them and they both ducked out of sight.

'Did he see us?' hissed Ron.

'I dunno.'

They both peered through the bushes without their binoculars and saw the two cleaners wandering in the direction of the factory.

Ron returned his attention to Molly and James, grabbed his binoculars and zoomed in on Molly, who was holding a champagne bottle. 'This is it.'

Fred followed suit and they both watched as Molly proceeded to remove the foil from the top of the bottle.

Fred was about to list the litany of low-level Health and Safety breaches that Molly was committing but decided against it - the visual evidence would be proof enough.

POP! With the approximate force of one hundred and sixty newtons the offending champagne cork flew into the air.

In the same indeterminable location in time and space the PLOTLINE monitoring system was having a busy time of it. This increase in workload was being caused by the cluster-novelty time travel happening in the vicinity of the Thurrock factory on the planet Earth, and by the fact that the planet Zoogos was holding its annual Tempus Fugit Competition, which involves eccentric Zoogonians attaching themselves to all kinds of ingeniously designed temporal generators, hurling themselves off the end of a wooden walkway, which extends over a stretch of water, and getting very wet. This competition has not, up to this temporal point, resulted in a device capable of time travel, but without fail it creates glitches in the Wave of Temporalati which nevertheless must be monitored.

Not to mention the background monitoring of the regular incursions into the Wave of Temporalati by the inhabitants of such planets as Castos, who have been flitting around in time for aeons and realise the importance of official channels and filing a flight plan.

The alarm sounded, numerous retro-screens flashed up the word ALERT and the soothing voice re-iterated the sentiment. 'Alert, PLOTLINE monitoring system activated. Detecting fluctuations in the Wave of Temporalati. Time travel confirmed. Origin: the 11th of October 2018…' This was as far as the soothing voice got before it was interrupted by a higher-pitched alarm. 'Alert, Domino Directive override. Domino Directive override. Monitoring of specific event aborted.'

Fred and Ron exchanged an enquiring look as the faint, unmistakable whoosh-wash sound of a time beam depositing someone or something nearby sounded. Perhaps their Health & Safety supervisor had arrived to check on their progress and make sure they weren't stringing the mission out. They decided that if this was the case, their best course of action was to look busy, so they started conducting a thorough inventory of their equipment.

Ron sounded less gruff. 'I reckon we've got preliminary, incontrovertible evidence that Sara 'primary-subject' Wright has inherited high-risk DNA from her grandmother.'

A young woman's voice asked, 'What's my daredevil grandmother up to now?'

Fred and Ron whirled round, instantly recognising the lithe, athletic young woman addressing them.

'Sara Wright!' Fred blurted out in horror.

Fred and Ron glared at their primary subject. She had made no attempt to merge into the era as they had done, in fact she drew attention to her time traveller status by wearing a T-shirt with 65 emblazoned on the front. Over which she wore a grey cropped jacket: cropped, they had ascertained on their earlier evidence gathering mission, to allow her ease of access to the two sizeable handguns

56

resting in the holsters which she wore round her waist over a pair of rugged, sand-coloured combat trousers.

Finally, Fred spoke up, 'You shouldn't be here, it will invalidate our pre-emptive Health & Safety evaluation mission.'

'What on earth's that?' queried Sara.

'We can't speak to you,' Ron informed her, returning to itemising his equipment.

'Domino directive,' stated Sara.

Ron bowed his head and muttered, 'No.'

Fred looked startled. 'Are you serious?'

Sara nodded.

Ron, his worst fears realised, rested his head on his flight case and groaned. 'I've always said signing the Domino Directive clause was a bad move.'

Fred, throwing caution to the wind, stuffed his gloves into his flight case and slammed it shut. 'But we didn't have a choice, did we? We're not members of the upper Senate and we haven't got a medical exemption certificate. And it has its benefits,' he added.

'Like what?' mumbled Ron.

'We might get to see something more exciting than two people having a picnic.'

'You know I don't like excitement,' Ron reminded him.

Sara studied the two weirdly-dressed men; she was beginning to have serious doubts about their usefulness on her mission. 'Do I need to remind you of subsection 1-31 of the Domino Directive? And I quote, "In the event of the Domino Directive being activated, this supersedes all other…" '

' "…assignments, obligations, missions…" ' Fred interrupted. 'We know every syllable of it. What's the exigency?' he asked, not sure why he was using such a cumbersome word. He had a sneaking suspicion that his subliminal ego was feeling threatened by this young, fearless, adrenaline-fuelled woman, who was everything he wasn't.

Unfazed, Sara continued, 'Non-terrestrial energy signatures have been detected in this area.'

Ron looked up. 'Is that all?' A glimmer of hope - now what was the subsection that dealt with avoiding the 1-31 clause?

Ignoring him, Sara continued, 'And we're authorised to use any and all means to neutralise any threats to the Earth.'

'I take back what I said about the 1960s,' said Fred.

'I've rigged up a tracking device in my sports car,' Sara informed them. 'Come on!'

Ron felt a leaden gloom sink onto his shoulders as he watched Sara sprinting off over the field towards a five-bar gate in the distance. 'Sports car,' he exclaimed, dismayed.

Fred grabbed his flight case and, realising he didn't have time to faff around folding up his terrain-adaptive chair, he darted off after Sara.

A despairing Ron looked from the abandoned chair to Fred's retreating figure in disbelief.

Chapter 9.

'*You just have to look at Sara's choice of sports car to know she's related to Molly*,' thought Fred, as he approached the sleek, racing green, open-top sports car.

'Shove your stuff in the boot, Fred,' Sara said, sliding into the driver's seat.

Fred somehow managed to squeeze his sizeable flight case into the boot which already contained Sara's equipment - a bulging rucksack with the butts of two serious-looking machine guns poking out, and a rope ladder. He then joined Sara in the front of the car. 'Where's Ron going to sit?'

'Don't worry, I've had the car modified so that there's space for one more,' she replied.

Fred looked at the tiny seat in the back of the car. '*Ron is not going to be happy*,' he thought.

Sara switched on the tracking device, which was piggybacking off the radio, which was playing something about shaking your hippy-hippies. The tracking device, mounted on the dashboard, located the non-terrestrial energy signatures and Sara was keen to get going.

Ron arrived with an overdramatic groan, sweat glistening on his brow. He had been determined not to let his standards slip under any circumstances and had trudged across the field, his flight case slung over his shoulder and an open terrain-adaptive chair in each hand. He placed the chairs down, gave one of them a quick weight-bearing test and sat down, glaring at the occupants of the car.

Sara started the car's powerful engine.

'I'm not travelling in that death trap,' Ron insisted.

Sara glared back at him. 'This is an E-type Jaguar Series One Roadster.'

'So?' grumbled Ron.

'It's the pinnacle of 1960s automotive engineering.' She revved the engine. 'A 4.2 litre hunk of an engine, which generates 265 horsepower and a cruising speed of 150mph. Sleek with a dash, for us, of retro-vibe and for the 1960s an ultra-modern space age vibe.'

Ron sat his ground. 'No seatbelts or headrests. The crumple-impact zone looks impressive but is non-existent.' He folded his arms and scowled at Sara. 'Need I go on?'

'Subsection 1-31,' said Sara.

During his long trudge across the field, Ron had accessed his Domino Directive contract on the screen of his goggles and had scoured it for any unacceptable risk to person clause but had come up with diddly-squat. Realising he couldn't moan himself out of this one without getting sued, with very bad grace, he painstakingly started to fold one of the chairs.

Fred could see that Sara was losing her patience; not something you want a person with two easily accessible sidearms, not to mention two high-velocity machine guns nearby, to do. 'Just leave the chairs, Ron,' he barked.

Stunned by his partner's gruff outburst, Ron complied, somehow wedging himself and his flight case into the minuscule back 'seat' - if twenty centimetres of paddled, upholstered leather could be classed as a seat. He re-adjusted his protective eye wear. 'When I get back I'm booking an appointment to see my doctor.' He yawned. 'Sara, will you please resist the urge to follow the high-risk DNA tendencies you've inherited from your grandmother and…'

Sara grinned, executed a demon wheel spin and pulled away, drowning out the rest of Ron's request. Sara glanced into the rearview mirror and was surprised to see that Ron had dozed off. 'Have you guys had a tiring morning?' she shouted over the deep roar of the engine.

'No, he always falls asleep when faced with a dangerous situation,' Fred yelled, the increasing force of the wind threatening to snatch his words away. 'It's a skill he's developed over the years,' he informed her, his blond hair dancing in the slipstream.

'Ah, stress-induced narcolepsy. That's quite something.' Her doubts about Ron's usefulness on this mission confirmed. Sara was about to ask Fred how he felt about the current danger levels as she slipped down a gear to take a sharp bend but didn't bother when she saw the look of delight on his face.

Sara guided the E-type to a sedate stop in an area beside another five-bar gate. 'The energy signatures are coming from that field,' she informed Fred, taking the tracker out of its housing and springing out of the Jag.

Fred raked his fingers through his tangled hair, eased the passenger door open and staggered out of the car. Leaning on the gate he gazed across the field and took a calming breath; being driven at high speed along the narrow roads had certainly got his adrenaline pumping. 'I can't see anything.'

Sara grabbed her rucksack from the boot. 'I imagine it will be an underground base as there doesn't seem to be any evidence of a crash site.' She vaulted over the fence and headed off with the tracker.

Ron shifted. He yawned and attempted to stretch. He was used to waking up in unusual places and knew he could rely on Fred to make sure that he was safe. He unfolded his legs and stretched. Opening his eyes, he could see billowing white clouds floating across the sapphire sky. A niggling question wafted into his brain - where was Fred?

Ron found Fred and Sara standing in the middle of the field, hunched over the tracking device.

'We're right on top of it,' remarked Sara, taking off her rucksack and rummaging around in it.

'How do we get in?' asked Fred, keen for some more action.

'No idea,' she replied. Suddenly the ground gave way and she plummeted downwards, leaving behind a surprised-looking Fred and Ron.

Ron saw his chance. 'Right, that's it: the perfect get-out clause. Let's leave her to it.'

'We can't just abandon her!' Fred fumbled to switch on the integral lights on his goggles and leant over the hole. 'Goodness knows how far down it goes.'

'I have no intention of finding out.'

'Look, Ron, if I'd fallen down a chute into what is presumably an alien base, you'd come after me - right?'

'Wrong.'

Fred swung his legs over the side of the chute and clasped his arms to his chest. 'Are you sure?' And with that he disappeared down the hole.

Ron threw himself to the ground and shouted down the hole, 'Alfred!'

The sound of his increasingly wayward colleague whooping in delight reverberated back to him, followed by an ominous crump, and silence.

'Fred?!' Nothing. Muttering unpleasantries under his breath, he headed off in the direction of Sara's car. He couldn't quite believe what he was contemplating - a daring rescue mission involving considerable personal danger. He stifled a yawn and diverted his mind by picturing himself leafing through his precious stamp collection. On reaching the sports car he opened his flight case and took out two sets of devices. He occasionally used one of the devices to pick up metal items that, having been dropped, invariably ended up in the most inaccessible place possible, but he had never, ever used them for the purpose they were designed for. His fellow Health & Safety experts had nicknamed them Spiderman pads and considered them 'best avoided.' He called them Death pads, short for 'devices likely to fail at an inopportune moment and result in one plunging to one's death pads' and obviously never considered using them at all.

Now here he was strapping the larger pair to his knees. Perhaps he was suffering from the early signs of temporal trauma, he reasoned.

Reaching the opening to the chute, Ron activated the magnetic fields on both sets of devices and placed one of the handheld devices onto the wall of the chute - the magnetic integrity readout confirmed that the magnetic seals weren't compromised by the composition of the chute's metal. He rolled over onto his front so that he could lower his legs into the chute and felt himself dropping off to sleep. Desperate not to fall asleep, Ron activated the screen on his safety goggles and selected his favourite viewing material: close-up footage of every single stamp in his collection, with the added bonus of his own fascinating commentary. He lowered his legs into the chute; with a clang his knees attached themselves to the metallic wall and at a snail's pace he edged his way down.

At the bottom of the chute, Fred's recumbent form stirred. A strange rhythmic clanging was forcing his unconscious mind to surface. Gathering his thoughts, he sat up and with a soft whirl of energy the corridor within five meters of his location was illuminated. He took in his surroundings: a sizeable tunnel clad with some kind of silver-coloured, lightweight metal - judging by the dent he - and presumably Sara - had made when they'd impacted the far wall, and a walkway which led off to his right.

'Sara?' he called. Spotting her abandoned rucksack close by, he opened it and whistled when he saw the contents: a number of what appeared to be explosive devices.

By now the clanging was getting closer and was definitely coming from the chute. Fred smiled. 'Is that you, Ron?'

'Who else would it be?' came the terse, muffled reply.

'Well, get a move on.'

'Don't push it, Fred.'

'I knew I could rely on my old mate.'

The soles of Ron's safety boots appeared at the rim of the chute, followed by Ron's hi-vis form. 'I reckon we've got self-certificating grounds for opting out of the Domino Directive.'

'How come you didn't fall asleep?'

'I did! Even the vid of my stamp collection couldn't stop me from dozing off; that's why it took me so long.' He gazed down the unappealing tunnel. 'Where's Sara got to?'

Fred stood up and gently put Sara's rucksack over his shoulders. 'She's vanished.' He reached forward to give Ron a hand up. 'Come on.'

'Could this situation get any worse?'

'Knowing Sara's DNA as we do, the obvious answer to that is "oh, yes".'

Chapter 10.

As Fred and Ron made their way down the tunnel, the system of motion-activated lights continued to illuminate their immediate path along the metal gantry, giving Ron the opportunity to list the numerous Health and Safety issues present in their current working environment. He had gone into his standard, monotone reporting voice, '...non-continuous low-level lighting which, whilst being energy-efficient, creates trip hazards and overhead hazards. Raised entry to doorways/ hatches creating trip hazards on entry and egress...'

'Alright, Ron,' snapped Fred. 'I get it. We've got to use our brains and go steady.'

'That remark has wiped out everything we hold to be sacrosanct,' complained Ron.

An overhead outlet pipe expelled a puff of smoke making Fred and Ron cough and splutter. Ron was about to say something derogatory about air pollution particles when, up ahead, they both spotted a heavy metal hatch. Above it was a sign written in an alien language. They both stared at the sign through their goggles and waited for them to translate the words. CHAMBER CORE HAZARDOUS ENERGY scrolled across the interior of their goggles.

'Energy core chamber - hazardous,' suggested Fred, guessing that the aliens had a tenuous grasp on the generative syntax of the English language.

Ron sighed. 'Judging by the sketchy grasp of Health and Safety issues shown by the occupants of this base, that must mean whatever's behind that door is so unimaginably dangerous it doesn't bear thinking about.' Ron moved to his left and the lights hummed into action, revealing a circular walkway leading around the edge of what looked like the hub of the base.

Fred continued to focus on the heavy metal hatch: after all, they were searching for a person who would instinctively gravitate to hazardous locations. He let his goggles translate the words on the opening mechanism and pressed the OPEN button. The hatch swung open, revealing a short corridor lined with a denser, heavy-duty form of cladding. He headed down the corridor towards the next hatchway. 'Come on, Ron.'

The hatch swung open and an arid, intense heat hit them. Fred, followed by a reluctant Ron, stepped carefully over the raised entry point and they cautiously made their way into the cavernous, dome-shaped chamber. They stopped, relieved, as the outline of Sara came into view.

There was one slight problem, though: Sara was tied by her ankles and dangling upside down over the circular energy core embedded in the floor at the centre of the chamber.

Fred rushed towards her. 'Sara!'

'Hi.'

Ron gazed up at Sara, noticing the patchwork of silver and black tiles which lined the dome above her, presumably designed to absorb and recycle the excess energy created by whatever form of power conversion this core processed. 'You look like you've got yourself into a precarious situation.'

'Dangling over the active manifold of a neutronic energy core is more of an inconvenience, really,' said Sara, underplaying the dire nature of her situation with a degree of *savoir faire* her grandmother would have been proud of.

'We'll leave you to it then,' said Ron, already beginning to feel weak and dizzy in this inhospitable environment.

'Some assistance would be appreciated,' remarked Sara.

Fred and Ron, in perfect unison, breathed in sharply through narrowed lips, shook their heads and set off at a slow, measured pace in opposite directions around the raised access port to the energy core. Hands clasped behind their backs, they surveyed the area.

Sara twisted round towards Fred, 'Although I enjoy having my spine stretched,' began Sara, 'it is getting rather painful, and not to mention hot, up here.'

Fred frowned and looked up at her. 'I'm sorry Sara, but we have to do a comprehensive inspection of the hazard area in correlation with any potential risk-related actions, and fully assess and evaluate the level of risk to our persons,' he recited, adopting the same monotone delivery employed by Ron earlier, although quite a bit louder.

If Sara hadn't been focusing on zipping up her core muscles, imagining that she was doing a strenuous Pilates session in the sauna with the added bonus of blood circulation therapy and lymphatic drainage, she would have asked Fred if he'd received special vocal training to dampen the modulation of his delivery, but reverse locational diversion of the brain requires concentration, so she didn't bother.

'And I don't want to be pessimistic, but I think you'll agree with me, Ron,' continued a pensive Fred, 'when I say that Sara's current predicament and the likelihood of an expedient rescue is level six on the USELESS induction manual scale.'

'Useless scale?' squawked Sara, her *sangfroid* evaporating as the energy core rumbled and expelled a scorching funnel of noxious particles.

'The Universal Safety Executive's Legislation… er… something, something,' said Ron, beginning to feel very dizzy. 'And I'd say more like…oh… level eight,' he concluded, as they both completed their one hundred and eighty degree perusal and stood face to face.

'That bad, eh?' said Fred.

'Well, maybe nine or ten,' said Ron, staggering towards the inner hatch and the relative coolness of the corridor. 'Which, as you know, Fred, means I'm going to have to lie down.'

'Yeah, but what about earlier, when you came to my rescue?' asked Fred, following him.

'That was a once in a lifetime aberration, mate.'

'Fair dos,' said Fred.

'Will you two stop messing around and do something - now!' yelled Sara, the unpleasant smell of the searing heat singeing her ponytail wafted up towards her.

'Hang on, Sara,' called Fred, 'just got to let Ron get settled and I'll be right with you.' He removed Sara's rucksack and placed it under Ron's head. 'There you go, mate, sweet dreams.'

'Wake me up when it's over.' And with that Ron slipped into a deep sleep.

The core roared and fizzed.

'FRED!' beseeched Sara.

'Just give him a couple of seconds,' Fred shouted, removing his sweat-drenched tunic to reveal a sweat-drenched, flamboyant white ruffled shirt.

The core rumbled and sent red sparks whizzing up towards Sara. 'What are you on about?!'

'Well, I've never told Ron but he sleepwalks and, fortunately, his subconscious is highly susceptible.'

At that moment a blinding flash shot out from the access port of the neuronic energy core, and through his protective goggles Fred could see that Sara was in serious danger of being vaporised. 'Right!' yelled Fred, psyching himself up. 'Ron!'

Ron sat bolt upright. His eyes shot open and stared at Fred.

Fred yanked Ron to his feet, 'Follow me and blink every five seconds,' he instructed Ron, mindful of the first time he'd discovered Ron's unusual ability and his mate had ended up with damaged corneas.

The two men darted through the inner hatch and raced up the stairs which hugged the outer wall of the chamber.

An astonished Sara watched as they reached the upper gantry that intersected the chamber and cluttered towards her.

Fred and Ron stopped at the safety barrier which encircled Sara.

Fred studied the panel that controlled the pulley-system, which was holding Sara precariously over the ever-increasing energy buildup of the core.

Ron stood motionless, blinking as instructed.

Fred made a rapid assessment of the controls. Up and down were clearly marked, but he couldn't see a control to get Sara back to the gantry.

A massive surge of energy sizzled up towards Sara. 'Up, Fred!' implored Sara.

Fred activated the UP control and Sara moved out of immediate danger. Fred was relishing the incredible surge of energy that his autonomic nervous system was kindly producing; he felt indestructible. However, having spent his entire working life observing the foolhardy actions of others, problem-solving was not his forte. In fact, he was stumped. He stared at the control panel hoping that inspiration would strike, sweat glistening on his brow. He could hear Ron snoring and a dreadful feeling of helplessness churned his stomach. He glanced at Sara. He had to step out of his comfort zone. Tearing around in sports cars and throwing oneself down tunnels was tame. He had to find his personal danger zone and inhabit it - NOW!

He took two steps to the edge of the gantry and looked down at the swirling heart of the core. '*What's the most dangerous thing I can do?*' he thought. Then inspiration struck. He dashed back to Ron and guided him to the control panel. 'Ron, lower Sara down until I say stop,' he instructed. He placed Ron's hand on the lever, 'Up is up and down is down.' He went back to the edge and watched as Sara headed back down towards him. 'Ron, stop!' he yelled. Sara's arms were now level with his reach. 'Sara, start swinging; I'll grab you.' Removing his safety gloves, he gripped the handrail and leant out as far as he dared.

Sara looked doubtful. 'Fred, I'm beginning to think that this plan might be a little over-ambitious.'

Fred forced a smile. 'Don't worry, it will work.'

Sara reviewed her non-existent options and then started swinging back and forth. She finally gathered enough momentum to reach Fred's outstretched hand.

Fred grasped her hand and pulled her towards him. Inexplicably, at that precise moment the pulley mechanism jerked and Sara slipped downwards, only by half a metre, but it was enough to send Fred off balance. His grip on the handrail slipped, and he toppled over the edge.

Sara strained to take Fred's weight and grabbed his other hand.

A few seconds passed in an adrenaline-induced haze.

'That would have worked really well if it hadn't failed completely,' commented Sara.

Fred clung onto Sara, the pungent aroma of the anti-slip, high-durability, insulated soles of his safety boots melting drifted towards him. 'Argh,' he groaned, as his shoulders started feeling the strain.

'Tell me about it,' remarked Sara, trying to ignore the agonising pain in her shoulders.

'I can hear Ron saying, "Never undertake anything that is beyond your capabilities."' He glanced up at Ron and noticed a coil of rope on the floor of the metal gantry. 'Ron,' he called, 'take the rope at your feet, anchor it and…' He paused and looked up at Sara. 'There's something we've got to get straight first.'

'I'm not sure how much longer I can take this,' groaned Sara.

'Which hand are you going to grab the rope with?'

'Oh, yeah - I see what you mean. My right.'

'OK, my left,' he confirmed. 'Ron! Throw the rope to us now! My left, my left,' he muttered.

Unflinching, Ron stood right at the edge of the gantry and threw the rope at them. By some miracle they both caught it.

'Alright,' shouted an elated Fred.

Sara echoed his jubilation with an exhausted, 'Alright.'

'Ron, heave us in, mate.'

With a degree of strength belying his slight muscular frame, Fred's sleeping partner hauled them back to the relative safety of the gantry.

Sara and Fred collapsed in a heap at Ron's feet and took some deep, calming breaths.

'I can see why you love all this high-risk activity,' said Fred, reaching over to untie Sara's ankles.

Sara eased herself into a seated position, gently rotated her aching shoulders and brushed her matted hair off her forehead. 'I think we need to hydrate.'

With Ron in tow, Sara and Fred made their way down the stairway.

'Did you actually talk to these aliens?' Fred asked Sara.

'Not exactly,' she replied. 'I came to at the bottom of the chute, heard some footsteps approaching so I pretended to be unconscious. From what they were saying, they're on a mission to assess the Earth's defences, and they didn't sound very impressed.' They reached ground level and headed towards the inner hatch.

'What did you do next?'

Sara smiled. 'I pretended to come round and they zapped me. Next thing I know I'm dangling over the core.'

'Did you see them? I mean what did they look like?'

'I got a glimpse.'

'And?'

'They were big, scary reptilian creatures who you wouldn't want with you on a ferry across the Mersey,' Sara informed him.

'Is that likely to happen?' asked a doubtful Fred.

'Well, aliens pop up in the most unusual places these days.'

The trio stepped through the inner hatch. Sara and Fred sank to the floor, relieved to be out of the intense heat.

'Ron, have a lie down,' instructed Fred.

Sara reached into her rucksack, pulled out two silver canisters and passed one to Fred. 'Drink up.'

They both gulped down the entire contents.

'And now?' asked Fred.

Sara contemplated their options. 'From what I could gather these aliens are an aggressive, combative race, so we're going to have to be hardcore in our approach.' She pulled out one of the compact, hexagonal devices from her rucksack.

'Is that what I think it is?' queried Fred.

'Well, I'm programming it for remote detonation; does that tally with your thoughts as to what it might be?'

'Yeah.'

Sara placed the primed device on the ground, stood up and poked her head into the chamber. 'We'll place,' she looked round the chamber calculating the cubic area and the corresponding yield required, 'um…six of these on the outer walls.' She returned to her rucksack, took out five more devices and started to programme them. 'Then all we have to do is convince the aliens that if they don't leave the planet, we'll destroy the base.'

'Along with them and ourselves?'

'Yes.'

'Blimey, you don't mess around, do you?'

'Not when the future of the entire population of the Earth is at stake.' She passed Fred three of the primed devices. 'But we have to give them the option to leave peacefully.' She glanced at Ron. 'Is he ever going to wake up?'

'Oh, yeah, probably when we stop talking about blowing ourselves sky-high,' replied Fred, with a grin.

Chapter 11.

Situated in the much quieter, air-conditioned hub of the underground base was the command centre: a dimly-lit room lined with black panels on which streaming data scrolled down. An environmentalist may well have assumed that the aliens were endeavouring to keep their carbon-neutronic footprint as low as possible, but it had more to do with the fact that they were keen on remaining undetected by the inhabitants of the planet Earth.

One member of the aggressive, reptilian alien race encountered earlier by Sara stood in the centre of the room - an oppressive presence; in the most part this was due to its bulky, towering frame and, to a lesser degree, the crusty nature of its mottled green and grey skin; no amount of cosmetic surgery could make it look appealing even to its own kind. Not that it wanted to look appealing; this was Izar the commander of the Mydraxian Elite Invasion Viability Force. Nasty, ruthless, cruel and prone to bouts of shoutiness pretty much summed Izar up.

A diminutive alien fluttered around Izar, proving that even in a war-like race such as the Mydraxians there was the odd sensitive character who was not altogether happy with its work, skin texture or indeed life in general. This was Taarin the invasion coordinator, who was focused on successfully completing its required service with the Invasion Viability Force, so that it could return to its home planet and paint: oils, acrylic or zlug - Taarin hadn't decided yet.

It is interesting to note that the majority of higher-brained beings in the Multiverse have tended to evolve into bi-pedal, bi-upper-limbed life forms. This is, in the most part, due to the fact that in the early stages of their evolution they took great pleasure in chucking sticks and stones at each other and then running away. The Mydraxians were well into their chucking sticks and stones stage of development, with finely developed legs and arms, when their evolution was rudely interrupted by alien invaders. These alien invaders saw their war-like potential and press-ganged them into the feared ranks of their Intergalactic Attack Force. They compounded their error by accelerating the Mydraxians' evolution and generally tinkering with their DNA. Amongst other things, they heightened their aggressive instincts, introduced a protective, reptilian skin and secondary eye-guard. These actions came back to bite them on their well-toned butts when, a few centuries later, the Mydraxians rebelled and, in line with their augmented DNA, formed their own intergalactic attack force, wreaking havoc on large swathes of the Multiverse.

This protracted cycle of events has led to the ruthless members of the Elite Invasion Viability Force to always shoot first and never ask questions later and encouraged them to go around making other beings' lives as miserable as possible: a common maladjustment in the Multiverse.

A maladjustment that Izar relished, so much so that Izar spent a great deal of time shouting and growling at the crew, the majority of whom took the only expedient option available - they kept out of Izar's way. Izar glared at Taarin who, as invasion coordinator, didn't have that luxury. Izar's red and black marbled eyes shone through the apertures in its eye-guards. 'Report.'

Taarin, overcompensating for the maladjustment of its race, fluttered around some more waiting for the elusive science division to update it. At last the relevant data scrolled onto the screen. 'The pathogen has been refined according to your instructions. Its toxicity on homo sapiens has been increased.'

Izar's eye-guards shot open: a common reaction to anticipated victory amongst its race. The intensity of its marbled eyes increased. 'Prepare to release the pathogen into the planet's atmosphere.'

Taarin squared up to Izar and, much to Taarin's own surprise, it found itself puffing out its chest and generally trying to look more impressive. 'We must follow procedure and conduct a low-level test first, Commander.'

'Pah!' Izar snarled, leaning towards Taarin. 'We can test it on the entire population.'

'Procedure requires low-level testing,' Taarin reiterated.

Infuriated by the bureaucratic constraints placed on it in the field, Izar clenched its mottled, scaly fists and directed its aggression at the only being in the base who couldn't hide behind the multitude of rules and regulations that encumbered Izar: rules and regulations which had been placed specifically by a wise member of the Mydraxian race who recognised the maladjustment present in their society. And that one being was the Earthling currently experiencing lymphatic drainage therapy in the energy core chamber. 'Energy core visual,' Izar hissed at the computer which, whilst not being sentient, was technically available for venting aggression on, but Izar had tried it and had got nowhere. 'If the Earthling has survived...' Izar paused as the image on the screen revealed that Sara was no longer dangling over the energy core manifold.

'Perhaps the Earthling has been vaporised,' suggested Taarin.

As fastidious as it was aggressive, Izar growled, 'Locate the Earthling.'

The image on the screen switched to a view of Sara walking up a corridor, closely followed by Fred and Ron.

Izar's gruff demeanour changed to predatory delight. 'It would appear that these beings are more resourceful than we thought.' A thin smile spread across its face. 'Prepare bio-containment area D.'

Sara, Fred, and a well-rested Ron - although for some reason that he couldn't fathom, his arms and legs were aching - were heading along the curving corridor of what they assumed to be the hub of the base. They had gone past hatches labelled SCIENCE SECTION, LIVING SECTION, and STORAGE, but there was no sign of the command section. And no sign of any aliens; which struck Sara as odd.

'I don't think much of their security,' she said.

'Who cares, let's just get out of here,' said Ron.

Sara and Fred had managed to keep Ron awake by convincing him that they were going to find a safe way out of the base; one that didn't involve clambering up a chute. Although his griping was a pain, it compared favourably to having to give him a continuous stream of instructions - turn left, duck, step up...etc.

Their movement along the corridor activated the next bank of lights to reveal a heavy metal hatch on the outer wall of the corridor. They approached it and looked to see what it was, but there were no markings. Sensing danger, Sara said, 'I don't think that's it.'

Ron pushed past her. 'It might be a lift to the surface, come on!' He looked for an opening mechanism.

'Doesn't look like one to me,' said Sara, hanging back.

'Maybe it's voice activated,' muttered Ron. 'Open hatch,' he commanded, and with a hiss the hatch slid upwards to reveal a bare metal cubicle. 'Looks like one to me.' And he stepped inside before Fred could stop him.

The hatch slid shut and a voice announced, 'Bio-containment area sealed. Subject isolated.'

Sara rushed to join Fred who was trying to slide the hatch up whilst shouting, 'Open hatch, open hatch.'

'Preparing to release pathogen,' stated the voice.

In the control room Izar watched as the events unfolded, its eyes blazing with anticipation. 'Command computer - open bio-containment capsule viewport.'

In the corridor a small screen on the hatch opened to reveal a bemused looking Ron. The fact that he wasn't fast asleep led Fred to reason that Ron must be oblivious to the danger he was in.

'Sara! Do something,' pleaded Fred.

Sara reached into her rucksack and pulled out her high-velocity machine guns. 'Get back, Fred,' she yelled, taking aim at the viewport.

Fred gestured at Ron to duck and retreated. He watched in despair as the bullets hit the 'glass' and were absorbed into the translucent liquid material.

Sara stopped firing. The sound of pressure building up in the area above the cubicle drew her attention to a large pipe running around the exterior, upper section of the cubicle. Passing her machine guns to Fred, she unclipped one of her handguns from its holster. Taking careful aim she let off one round, which pierced the pipe.

'Warning, integrity of bio-containment capsule compromised. Dispersal of pathogen aborted. Emergency decontamination of area D proceeding.'

In the control room Izar shouted at the computer, 'Negative, continue. Release the pathogen!'

But the computer's safety protocols were locked in, and it would take more than an irate commander to override them.

In the corridor amongst the sound of air being extracted and filtered air returning, the hiss of the bio-containment hatch opening was heard and a sheepish-looking Ron emerged. 'Not a lift then,' he remarked.

Izar scowled at the image of the three Earthlings. 'They are a threat. They must be destroyed.'

Taarin could feel its chest puffing out again. 'These are the first Earthlings to have made any attempt to resist our presence on their planet. My Invasion Viability Assessment would be incomplete if I do not speak with them.'

The green-grey tinge of Izar's skin turned puce and Taarin wondered if it had gone too far.

'All I need to know is that their defences are insignificant and puny,' Izar snarled. '**My** Invasion Viability Report is complete and ready for transmission.'

'Part of my role is to categorise the intelligence of all sentient beings on this planet and if the dominant life form is above level C1, the council will be unlikely to agree to invasion.'

'Hah!' exclaimed Izar, making it clear what it thought of Taarin's contribution to the mission. 'These dominant lifeforms still kill each other with projectile weapons and they've only just harnessed the power of basic nuclear weapons.'

Taarin met Izar's gaze calmly. 'When I know what their intentions are, I will make my final evaluation of their intelligence levels.'

'Why the Invasion Council thinks that the intelligence of lesser species is relevant alludes me.'

'That's why I'm here.'

Moving towards Taarin, Izar pulled out the bulky sidearm that it carried at all times.

'Perhaps I should mention, Commander, that if I fail to embed my personal verification code into the data stream of the Invasion Viability Report, the computer will automatically transmit the extensive report that I have compiled about your disregard for official procedures.'

Izar clamped shut its secondary eyelids, took a deep breath, and tilted its head back.

The tension in the air was palpable as Taarin waited, unsure if the Commander was preparing to back down or shoot.

At that precise moment the main hatch to the control room slid open and the three Earthlings entered the room.

'This isn't the way out,' exclaimed Ron, immediately ducking back out of the room, which was fortunate because Izar let out a tremendous roar and fired. The bolt scorched the bulkhead where moments earlier Ron had been standing.

Izar then took aim at Sara.

'Sorry to barge in, but we need a word,' said Sara.

Taarin stepped forward, blocking Izar's line of fire. 'Proceed.'

Sara held up the remote detonator. 'I must inform you that we have placed high explosives in the energy core chamber…'

Ron appeared at the hatchway. 'What's she on about?' he whispered to Fred.

'Shh, Sara knows what she's doing.'

Taarin turned to Izar. 'I'm thinking intelligence level C9.'

Izar grinned - how it loved to be proved right.

Sara, trying to keep a grip on the situation, sternly offered the aliens their ultimatum. 'And if you don't leave our planet immediately, I won't hesitate to detonate them.'

'Then you would be destroyed too,' stated Izar.

'Yes,' replied Sara.

'Or perhaps D4,' said Taarin, its intelligence rating of these beings tumbling.

Izar lowered its sidearm. 'Very well, do it.'

'Izar! Don't antagonise them. My final evaluation is level D4,' said Taarin.

'I want to see if they will carry out their threat,' growled Izar.

'Are you sure she knows what she's doing, Fred?' asked Ron.

'Shouldn't you be asleep by now?'

'I seem to be suffering from insomnia. I think it must be adrenaline overload,' he replied.

Sara glanced over at her two companions, a look of sadness in her eyes. 'I had hoped that it wouldn't come to this.' She pressed the button on the remote detonator. Nothing.

Izar glowered at her.

She gave the device a quick shake, then pressed the button again. Nothing.

'Perhaps I should have mentioned that your device will not function within the confines of our control room,' Izar said, smirking.

Sara darted for the hatch but Ron, who was still standing in the hatchway, wasn't quick enough; or maybe he wasn't very keen on being blown up. Whichever, the upshot was that Izar had ample time to stun Sara and, for the second time that morning, she achieved the unenviable distinction of impacting a wall in the underground base.

Izar stomped over and stamped on the remote activator, which had fallen from Sara's grasp. It looked down at Sara. 'We appear to have our test subject for the pathogen.' With a hiss Izar turned its attention to the two other Earthlings. Fred and Ron responded by taking a non-aggressive stance, which involved staring at the toecaps of their boots.

'Feeble beings,' sneered Izar. Grabbing one of Sara's arms, it dragged her towards another bio-containment capsule tucked away in the far corner of the control room and deposited her inside.

Fred and Ron exchanged a desperate look as the hatch slid shut. Then Ron stepped forward, cleared his throat and said, 'Of course, wiping us out with a deadly pathogen will be simple,' his voice wavering as Izar took aim with its blaster. 'But have you considered the cleanup operation?' Ron rattled off his question in double quick time, then closed his eyes expecting to be stunned. Nothing happened so he opened his eyes and continued, 'I mean what about all those germs?'

'Explain,' said Taarin.

'Well, it's obvious, isn't it? Billions of dead bodies left lying around the place will cause a terrible health risk, wouldn't you say, Fred?'

'Oh yes, doesn't bear thinking about. All those decomposing bodies - nasty.'

Ron nodded. 'The water supply would be compromised...'

Izar whirled round, 'You're not listening to these fools, are you?'

'I categorise these Earthlings as borderline C1,' countered Taarin. 'If you don't let me listen to them, I will be forced to trigger a Supreme Council review of this Invasion Viability Mission.'

Izar looked like it was about to suffer an apoplectic seizure. 'You would not dare?!'

Fred and Ron exchanged a worried look and reverted to inspecting the toecaps of their boots.

'Yes, I would dare!' hissed Taarin.

There was a protracted silence. The two aliens scowled at each other.

'Very well, listen to them.' The words spat from Izar's lips. 'Speak!' it ordered the humans, turned about heel and left the control room, presumably to go and make another member of its errant crew's life a misery.

A flustered Ron gathered his wits, 'Yes, hum…well…then there's the 'War of the Worlds' scenario.'

'Oh yes,' concurred Fred. 'When alien invaders were wiped out by nothing more dangerous than the common cold.'

'Exactly, have you considered that you might be wiped out by…' Ron paused, trying to think of a comparable virus.

'A verruca,' interjected Fred, who had no such qualms about medical accuracy.

Taarin scrolled through the Invasion Viability Report on a nearby screen: it didn't like the sound of verruca at all. 'The science division haven't made any reference to such a possibility.'

'Well, I think you should,' advised Ron. 'It would be a shame if you were to wipe out the entire population of the planet and engage in a costly, time consuming cleanup operation; only to find that your species is eradicated by a virus that we contract from walking around swimming pools.'

'I shall add it to the report,' confirmed Taarin.

Ron pressed on, his confidence increasing. 'Then there's the nuclear catastrophe scenario.'

'Explain,' said Taarin.

Dredging through his pre-mission background research into the 1960s. 'What do you know about Magnox reactors?'

Taarin glanced up at Ron. 'Our preliminary assessment is that they are of a primitive, inefficient design.'

'Indeed, and did you know that the reactors have a tendency to experience fatigue failure and...well...blow up? Periodic safety checks are a must. Do you know how to conduct a safety evaluation?' he asked.

A concerned Taarin continued to revise the report. 'Do you have any other relevant information?'

Ron glanced at Fred, he'd run out of plausible recommendations.

'We've nearly depleted the Earth's natural resources. You could go for solar power, but that could take over fifty years to recoup the initial outlay.'

'Yes,' Ron had thought of something else, 'did you know that the magnetic poles of this planet switch every so often? I mean in a hundred and fifty years you'll have just got used to saying: "I'm popping up to Manchester today," when ping! the poles switch and it's: "I'm popping down to Manchester." And you'll have to start saying: "It's grim up south, northerners are soft..."'

Fred gave him a sharp elbow in the ribs and whispered, 'Don't overdo it, mate.'

'Is that any help?' Ron asked.

'You have been most forthcoming, thank you. I have updated my section of the Invasion Viability Report. Computer, transmit encoded data stream to the Invasion Viability Council,' instructed Taarin.

'Transmitting,' confirmed the computer.

A dull thudding drew their attention to the bio-containment booth. In all the excitement they'd forgotten about Sara.

Taarin opened the hatch.

A dazed Sara emerged. 'Have I missed anything?'

Chapter 12.

A while later Sara was beginning to wish she hadn't asked. Ron had proceeded to give her a blow-by-blow account of their Health and Safety risk assessment on invading the planet Earth, but as he concluded his recitation, she could see that it was an ingenious ruse that might, just, if they were lucky - work.

'You guys are amazing,' enthused Sara, giving the two men a big hug.

'Who said Health and Safety is useless?' said Ron.

Sara smiled. 'The thought never crossed my mind.'

'How long do you think it will take the Invasion Council to reach a decision?' Fred asked Taarin.

'Unknown, I'm afraid,' Taarin replied. 'I believe they have twenty viability reports pending.'

'Twenty!' exclaimed Fred.

'In that case,' began Ron, 'may I take the opportunity to give you some free, impartial advice on the implementation of good working practices in your current working environment?' He was keen to take his mind off the potentially devastating decision being discussed by a group of faceless bureaucrats in a galaxy an unknown distance away.

Taarin nodded. If anything could divert its mind from the current stress of their situation, it was impartial advice on the implementation of good working practices in its current working environment. Taarin picked up a portable data device.

'My first recommendation is to clearly mark any trip hazards, overhead hazards, and machinery that is not intrinsically safe.' He paused to allow Taarin sufficient time to make notes. 'On this point, I further advise that signage should be used to state the level of hazard present. A sliding scale of one to ten is recommended...'

Sara nudged Fred. 'How long will this take?'

Fred grinned. 'You'd better get comfortable.'

Sara sat down on the floor, took one of her high-velocity machine guns out from her rucksack and proceeded to check the firing mechanism.

Ron looked pointedly at her. 'Firearms are prohibited at all times.'

Sara gave him a mock scowl and put the gun away. She stretched out her legs, leant back against the bulkhead and closed her eyes - she had to come up with a backup plan in case the Invasion Council was not fooled by the creative nature of the points raised by Fred and Ron.

Fred was wandering around the control room, passing the time by glancing at the various control panels.

'Under no circumstances may any device, control, or equipment be operated without prior agreement from the relevant authorities - Fred!'

Fred snapped out of his reverie. 'Stepping away from everything, Ron.'

Ron was about to launch into his minimising environmental risk to health recommendations, when a high-pitched alarm sounded.

'That will be the verdict,' Taarin informed them.

Leaping to her feet, Sara said, 'That was quick; is that good or bad?'

'Impossible to say,' replied Taarin, activating the central screen. The word STANDBY materialised.

Sara, Fred and Ron exchanged nervous looks as they waited to hear the fate of their planet.

The word STANDBY dissolved and the letters DNI formed on the screen. The three humans looked quizzically at Taarin.

'Do not invade!'

The three residents of the planet Earth demonstrated their relief and jubilation by laughing, jumping up and down, and making quite a spectacle of themselves.

Up to this point the wisdom of this particular universe had been keeping things ticking along nicely.

Above ground Myrtle, Maud, and their keep-fit class were in the midst of warm-down stretches; Molly and James were discussing the relative merits of responsible drinking; and the rest of the population of the planet were going about their business unaware of the near miss.

Below ground, in its infinite wisdom, the Multiverse added a new, improved layer of incipient complexity to the proceedings: known to the inhabitants of the Earth as the 'it ain't over 'til it's over' principle.

With a tremendous crash, the entire underground base shook and everyone was thrown to the floor as a blast of energy surged through the structure. The base was flooded with bright light as the auto-systems diverted the energy overload into the nonessential circuits of the lighting grid and then the computer stacks deep within the substructure of the base exploded as it all became too much, and the control room was plunged into an eerie iridescent light.

'What the hell was that?!' yelled Sara, springing to her feet, high-velocity guns at the ready.

Taarin rushed over to the nearest readout panel and tried to make sense of the intermittent script sputtering down the panel. The backup systems had kicked in but were struggling to counter the energy surge which was attempting to disable the primary systems.

The main hatch to the control room swung open and Izar stormed in. Throwing open a locker housed in the bulkhead, Izar reached in and handed Fred and Ron the alien equivalent of a high-velocity machine gun.

Taarin had abandoned its attempts to decipher the fragmented data on the readout panels and was scanning the immediate area with its portable data device. 'That's strange - there's an orange level energy surge being directed into the entire base. All primary systems are being disrupted.'

'Where's the source?' shouted Izar.

'It seems to be coming from…' An astonished Taarin looked down at the glowing red floor plating, '…there!'

Suddenly three humanoid figures burst through the metal plating and hovered in the cloud of particles displaced by their dramatic entrance.

Sara and Izar reacted first, blasting away. Then Fred joined in.

Ron fumbled with his gun, struggling to power it up. 'Help!' he called, but they all ignored him and continued shooting. However, their combined efforts were having zero effect as the volley of laser blasts and bullets just pinged off the three figures.

'Please note that your weapons are ineffective against our enhanced metallurgic exoskeletons. Please desist,' said one of the figures.

Amazed by the politeness of this being and realising that their weapons were indeed ineffectual, they threw their weapons down. In the background Taarin continued with its covert information gathering.

'Thank you for your compliance,' said another of the figures, although it was proving difficult to keep track of who was who amongst the uniformity of the figures: same height - tall, same build - bulky, same speech patterns - posh. On closer inspection they were each wearing an identical black protective armour. On even closer inspection the armour was crazed with tiny fractures which were full of sediment and what looked like sludge.

Sara was the first to click. 'Hang on, they're robots.'

'Correct,' they said in unison. 'We are Extraction Team Alpha.'

'How do you tell each other apart?' enquired Sara.

'It is not necessary to differentiate between units,' stated one of the robots. 'We must inform you, as the first representatives of the indigenous species of this planet that we have come into contact with, that the Magnostellar Mining Consortium has acquired the rights to extract the core of your planet.'

Stunned silence from the representatives of the indigenous species and their newfound allies. Finally, the three Earthlings uttered…

'Extract…'

'The core…'

'Of our planet…'

'Correct. A forcefield has been placed around the core. Mesotronic explosives have been placed outside the forcefield zone. Once detonated they will destroy the outer layers of the planet, facilitating efficient extraction.' One of the robots rattled off the stages to the stunned group.

Although Izar looked impressed and muttered, 'Nice plan.'

'Information download complete, please follow me.'

Even though Izar was impressed with the audacity of the Magnostellar Mining Consortium - in fact, Izar was envious: no time wasted on an invasion viability report, no deliberation by the Invasion

Council and no possibility of a Supreme Council review - Izar was less impressed by the fact that it, along with Taarin and the Earthlings, had been imprisoned in a bio-containment area. Squished would be a better way of describing their status: bio-containment areas are not known for their space and bio-contentment area B was no exception. Izar was even less impressed by the fact that it was about to be obliterated, along with the economically worthless outer layers of this rather militaristically desirable planet. The thought of its particles floating through the depths of the cosmos until they happened upon a black hole, or a star in the process of going supernova, did not lighten its mood.

Fred, sensing the despair emanating from his fellow prisoners, said, 'Come on everyone, we'll think of something.'

A hollow laugh from Ron. 'Oh yes, of course, Fred. All we have to do, with the vast array of alien technology to hand...' If he could he would have gestured at the total lack of anything within the bare walls of their confinement, but as he was pressed up against the outer wall there was no chance, '...is to build a device capable of tunnelling towards the Earth's core, which can also neutralise mesotronic explosives.'

Fred glared at him.

'Well it seems like a big ask to me, mate.'

'Listen, they're robots. Correct?' interjected Taarin.

'And?' said Fred.

'Designed to function in extreme conditions...' Taarin began, only to be interrupted by Ron.

'We can reprogram them.'

'No, we can incapacitate them so that they can't activate the explosives.'

'How?' asked Sara, perking up as an action plan took shape.

Taarin held its portable data device aloft and studied the information. 'According to my scans they operate on red-level energy cells, a base wide red-level energy surge should do it.'

'Should?' queried Ron.

'Will do it. We'll have to link the energy core to the endo-emitters, raise the energy core output to dangerous levels...'

'Then flood the base,' said Sara.

'Precisely.'

'Right, we need to get out of here.' Sara was back and looking for trouble.

'Hang on,' said Ron, not wanting to dampen the others enthusiasm but he could see a problem with the plan. 'What if these robots are like the field team and there's a command ship in orbit?'

Fred glared at him again.

'Just a thought.'

'No, you're right, Ron,' said Sara. 'Any ideas, Taarin?'

'If there is a ship, we can embed the red-level energy surge into a standard distress message and transmit it to the ship.'

Sara nodded. 'We really need to get out of here, now.'

Taarin pointed the portable data device at the hatch which, to everyone's amazement, slid open.

With the others having split up into pairs to achieve their designated goals - Taarin and Fred coordinating the red-level surge from the engineering section, and Izar and Ron overloading the energy core output - Sara headed off in the direction of the control room. As she made her way down the darkened corridor, she ran through her dazzling array of distraction techniques, pondering which would work best on robots.

Fred and Taarin arrived at the engineering section and stepped inside.

'Do you actually have any other crew on this base?' asked Fred.

'Yes, I imagine they're all locked up somewhere,' replied Taarin, activating one of the control panels so that Fred could locate any ships in orbit. 'Let's just hope we don't get interrupted.'

In the superheated energy core chamber Izar was busy bypassing the safety backup systems, which involved removing the linkages from the command control panel sited on the outer bulkhead. Izar would have preferred to smash the panel into a satisfying moosh of circuits, but even Izar knew that care should be taken when overloading the energy core.

Ron was on guard in the corridor outside the main hatch, which he was pleased about because he hadn't been looking forward to getting all hot and bothered in the energy core chamber.

Sara reached her destination last - the control room was the furthest away from their temporary prison and she'd crept along in the dark, half-expecting to meet other robots, which she hadn't; she assumed that the Magnostellar Mining Consortium must be on a tight budget.

She paused outside the hatch composing herself. She knew that she was about to try the oldest trick in the book when attempting to outwit robots - the good old logic paradox. Calling on every ounce of *sangfroid* she'd inherited from her grandmother, she opened the hatch and entered the control room.

One of the robots registered her intrusion with, 'You have escaped.'

Sara wandered into the room. 'I hope you don't mind, but the others were getting on my nerves. They're all stressing out for some reason.'

The other robot present commented, 'Organic species' emotional reactions to impending death are illogical.'

'And, to be honest,' Sara continued, 'I prefer the company of robots.'

'That is logical,' stated the unit to her left. 'Where are the other organic beings?'

'I locked them back in,' she said, and before the robots had the chance to process the improbability of her statement, she continued, 'I'm intrigued by your belief that the Earth's core is valuable.'

'It is not a belief, it is a fact,' stated the unit to her right. 'The Magnostellar Mining Consortium always conducts an economic feasibility study before employing our services.'

Sara took a deep breath, then went for it. 'Ah, yes, but would it not be logical to assume that, considering the consumer-driven, materialistic basis of our civilisation, we would have already utilised the vast wealth at their feet? Ergo, as we haven't, it's logical to conclude that the core of the Earth is worthless.'

Blank looks from the two robots, which of course meant nothing.

'Or, to put it another way, if it is not true that the Earth's core is not valuable, would it not be reasonable to conclude that your employers have ulterior motives? I don't know, maybe they want the Earth destroyed?' She looked at the robots. 'Would it not?' she added for good measure.

'Would what be not?' asked the unit to her right; fortunately, these two robots didn't feel the need to move around. *'One of the many advantages of being a non-organic being with a metallurgical exoskeleton,'* thought Sara, shifting her weight slightly. She was still feeling the odd twinge from the earlier overextension of her calcium-rich skeleton.

'Would what be not?' the unit to her right asked again.

'Oh, hmm… I'm not sure, I've lost my thread,' confessed Sara.

The unit to her left, having maintained its focus on Sara's meandering witterings, processed their flimsy veracity in all of five seconds. 'Data classified as irrelevant. Likely motivation of organic being: to create a logic, algorithm paradox in our command circuits. Reason: to divert our attention for motives of a covert nature. Proposition: to facilitate sabotage of our mission by the other organic beings.'

Sara looked pleased. Although her ruse had failed, she had managed to keep them occupied. She just had to hope she'd given the others enough time.

In the energy core chamber Izar had barely broken into a sweat thanks to its reptilian DNA. Extracting the final linkage, Izar looked round to see Ron sitting on the floor near the hatch. He was busy deactivating one of the explosive devices that Sara and Fred had planted earlier.

Sara watched as the two robots detected the fluctuating energy readings coming from the energy core.

'They have over-ridden the energy core safety circuitry,' stated the unit to her left.

'Any unit available proceed to the energy core chamber,' commanded the unit to her right.

In the engineering section Taarin had aligned the endo-emitters, and Fred had located a ghost energy signature, indicating a spaceship lurking in geostationary orbit.

All they could do was wait for the energy core to go critical.

A triumphant Izar stood by the raised access port to the energy core, watching the supraenergy vortex forming: a column of dense, death-grey atoms with ice-blue shards of energy shooting out, breaking free of their dreary compatriots. Izar glared at the core output readings and hissed with pleasure as the output levels edged towards the critical zone. Izar turned towards the Earthling, eager for someone to witness its moment of triumph - a small triumph it may be, but any victory, however small, should be relished.

Ron had entered the chamber and was walking around the energy core, mesmerised by the remarkable sight.

At that moment one of the robots appeared at the hatch and directed its attention towards Izar. 'You have escaped.'

Izar snarled with pleasure. So much more satisfying for a victory to be witnessed by the enemy, rather than by one's reluctant ally. 'Victory!'

The robot approached Izar. 'That statement is illogical, please clarify?'

Izar roared as the ice-blue shards of energy hit the black tiles lining the dome, which began to descend, intensifying the ice-blue storm of energy that surged around them.

'Danger,' stated the robot, 'energy core at critical levels. Immediate action required.' It raised its weapon and stunned Izar.

Ron peered round the rim of the energy core where he had taken cover and watched the robot replacing the linkages. He looked up and saw that the dome was returning its upper position, and the potency of the vortex fading. He had to do something, but he was hoping he wouldn't have to do the something he was thinking of doing. He stared at the explosive device in his hand: he had no choice. He decided to implement his plan in small stages - much easier on the nerves. One: he placed the explosive device on the floor. Two: he removed his hi-vis tunic, folded it neatly, placed it on the floor and retrieved the explosive. Three: he reactivated the device. Four: he crawled round the edge of the cowling to a point where he knew he'd have to break cover and muttered, 'I can do this.'

In the control room a despondent Sara watched as the robots countered their last-ditch attempts to save the Earth.

'The unit has reactivated the safety systems, automatic venting of elevated energy proceeding.'

'Command ship confirms core extraction procedures active and standing by. We are cleared to detonate.'

'All planet-based units prepare for detonation. Transmit final mission data. Oblivion imminent.'

It was at that moment that Sara realised why the Magnostellar Mining Consortium used robots: handy for doing all the hard, dangerous work, and they were dispensable.

Counterpointing the gradual decrease in activity in the energy core, Ron broke cover channeling all his race memory into a blood-curdling yell: a sound which all evolving organic species, especially bi-pedal ones with a fondness for chucking sticks and stones, would recognise.

Had the robot been an organic-evolving being it would have recognised the intent of such a noise, but needless to say it didn't. It stared at the wild-eyed human charging towards it. 'Query, why are you emitting this strange vocal emanation?'

Ron threw himself at the robot, clamping the explosive onto its back.

'Danger.' It flailed around trying to dislodge the device.

Ron, in between dodging the robot, stared in desperation at the safety linkages. For a moment he dithered, then he smashed the linkages with his fist.

This action caused three events intricately woven into the Wave of Temporalati to occur: the energy core went critical, Taarin initiated the red-level power surge, and Fred beamed out the distress call. Result: after a lot of fizzling and sizzling of circuits; in particular the circuits of the robots in the underground base and those on-board the command ship, the Earth's core, along with the outer layers of the planet, was safe.

Chapter 13.

A hatch in the field opened. A frazzled-looking Sara emerged. She stood swaying slightly then sunk to her knees and gracefully rolled onto the soft, cool grass. She gazed up at the beautiful blue sky, '*As outer layers of planets go, that has got to be one of the best,*' she thought. The sound of two men arguing drifted up the shaft. She smiled.

An unkempt Ron appeared at the top of the hatch. 'Are you sure?' he shouted back at Fred.

'Yes!' came Fred's terse reply.

Ron crawled a couple of feet along the grass and collapsed.

'Ron, you're not still going on about those explosives, are you?' asked Sara.

A dishevelled Fred appeared at the top of the hatch and grinned as he crawled out onto the ground.

'Well, what's the point in bothering to save the planet only to leave a load of active explosives around the core of said planet?' grumbled Ron.

'Taarin will sort it,' said Sara.

Overhead the distant rumble of the Mydraxians' space capsule heading through the ionosphere could be heard. 'They'll be docking at the Mining Consortium's ship soon. Izar will be strutting around surveying the 'prize' and pontificating about a glorious victory, which will give Taarin plenty of time to deactivate the bombs. End of.'

And with that reassurance they all drifted off into a well-earned snooze.

Time passed.

Domino objective achieved.

Multiverse contented.

An insistent beeping filtered into Fred's befuddled brain. He stirred, then he remembered that he'd set his reminder alert. 'We've got thirty minutes, Ron,' he called.

Ron groaned.

'I suppose you'll be heading back to file your report on my grandmother,' remarked Sara.

'Er, we haven't actually completed our assessment yet,' admitted Ron. 'We can definitely class her as reckless, but we need more proof.'

Fred sighed. The last thing he wanted to do right now was track down Sara's grandmother and gather evidence. He sighed again.

Ron glanced at Fred. 'I thought you wanted to check out Carnaby Street, Fred?'

'Well, yes!' Fred sat up. 'You mean go off the grid?' he said, astonished that Ron could even think of such a reckless course of action, let alone suggest it as a viable option.

'Yeah.' Ron settled back and closed his eyes. 'One of us has got to hang around for the mop-up team to arrive and close down this alien base. I can't be the only one having all the fun!'

'Cool, thanks, mate.'

Sara stood up. 'Sounds good to me, come on.' She threw the keys of her sports car to a delighted Fred.

Chapter 14.

By now it should be obvious that time travel isn't all it's cracked up to be. If you're fortunate enough to survive the experience, you'll either have no recollection of it happening, or you'll find yourself wandering up and down Carnaby Street as it dawns on you that the past is just as hectic, stressful and pungent as every other point in time. And no amount of groovy duds and chicks will change that fact. As the Xa of Sands puts it, "The insistent clamour that drowns out the death of hope prevails for all eternity."

The complex nature of time and travelling therein can be highlighted by the weird and wonderful connections that interlace the hessian substructure of the Multiverse; also known as temporal spacio-flux causality. A vivid example of which can be seen in the events focused around the Thurrock factory: on the crisp autumnal morning of the 11th October 1965, at exactly the same moment in time, two disparate groups of individuals: namely cleaning ladies and Thurrock's workers, and Health & Safety experts and a high-risk DNA relative of Molly Wright were, to varying degrees, getting hot and sweaty at different levels of the Earth's lithosphere. And, whilst this was happening, three notable events woven into the delicate fabric of the Wave of Temporalati were also occurring: in the galaxy known by the locals as the Milky Way, on the self-same life-supporting planet called the Earth, on a land mass situated to the western fringes of the continent of Europe, the Baker Street traffic lights on the intersection with the Marylebone Road turned red; in an office overlooking the Marylebone Road a worker polished the leaves on their cheese plant; and in a galaxy just round the corner a stellar cruiser orbiting another life-supporting planet engaged its phasic-shift generators...

The fact that these three notable events have nothing to do with keep-fit classes, the fate of the Earth's core, or the culinary tastes of two posh picnickers serves only to reinforce the incomprehensible nature the Wave of Temporalati, and indeed life in general.

If any sentient being had the patience and mental rigour necessary to examine the mass of data produced by the PLOTLINE monitoring system, they would discover that the causal tipping point of the bizarre antics focused round the Thurrock factory and Molly Wright was an apparently insignificant event that occurred on the 27th September 1965 - heavy rain was forecast for the southeastern corner of the previously-mentioned land mass known as Great Britain.

Pedants would argue at length that the causal tipping point was in fact either the birth of Molly Wright or that of Walter Kingdom Thurrock, the founder of the Thurrock empire. And ultra-pedants would, quite reasonably, if annoyingly, point out that it was the Big Bang.

Annoying because imagine, if you will, a time-travelling ultra-pedant meeting the Earth scientist Einstein just after he'd completed his painstaking research and had had a couple of apple-dropping-from-a-tree moments - otherwise known as the theory of general relativity and the theory of special relativity - and telling him that he couldn't have achieved this incredible feat if it hadn't been for a colossal surge of energy 13 billion years ago - which although being true on many levels, would take the edge off the joy of formulating two of the ten-and-a-half most revolutionary theories know to Earthlings.

Or the vast number of workers in the hospitality sector of the multi-economy, who after being nice and smiley **and** helpful the whole bloody time, discovered that they couldn't take any credit for the calm and tranquility that their professionalism imbued in others, and it belonged to what some beings see as a cosmic catastrophe which occurred aeons ago.

Ignoring the pedants and ultra-pedants, and taking the weather report as the primary causal tipping point, because it's a well-known fact that most beings in the Multiverse find it rather comforting to focus on weather predictions and all the decisions they force beings to make - an umbrella or a sun hat, shorts or trousers, sunblock or a dab of sun factor 10… probably because it saves them thinking too much about the nature of black holes and lazy matter, and why the lights at the Baker Street/Marylebone junction always turn red just as you reach them.

This particular forecast of heavy rain in the southeast of England was heard, amongst others, by Molly Wright, the trendy, self-assured, intelligent primary progenitor of all the action centred around the Thurrock factory. With an evening excursion to Surrey planned, she'd decided to leave work early, head home, and use the available time to revise and type up her comprehensive report on exciting job opportunities for women in the top secret organisation she worked for...or lack of them... and had switched the radio on to keep her spirits up. She glanced out of the large sash window which dominated the study-cum-library that she and her husband had sympathetically furnished in an elegant Victorian style - without the claustrophobic grandeur that the actual Victorians had been so fond of. Her eyes confirmed the weather forecast. '*Definitely gloomy and rather ominous*,' she thought.

Switching on the desk lamp, she returned to the least exciting part of her job - she clattered out her conclusion and pulled the final page out of the typewriter. She scanned the report. Satisfied, she placed it into a large brown envelope.

At that precise moment, the telephone rang. She picked up the receiver, 'Kensington 1571, Molly Wright speaking...' A slight smile played on her lips, 'Yes, I've just this minute finished it...I'll leave it in the usual place...My pleasure, goodbye.' She replaced the receiver into its cradle, picked up the envelope and licked the gum. She grimaced at the unusual taste, 'Oh, cough-drop flavour! Who on earth thought I'd appreciate a free sample of novelty-flavoured envelopes?' she muttered to herself, sealing the envelope.

The deep roar of a motorcycle speeding up the road alerted her to the imminent arrival of her fellow agent - James Harper. Rising from the desk, she headed towards the front door to welcome him. '*Bang on time as ever*,' she thought. She found James' impeccable manners reassuring, partly because they matched her own and had got them out of many a tricky situation, but mainly because they enabled her to plan her day with precision. Pausing in the hallway to execute a couple of pre-mission stretches, she opened the door just as James strolled up the path. James Harper, Esq. DFC wasn't exactly stuck in his heyday of the 1940s, but his penchant for tearing around on motorcycles had

94

enabled him to retain the style he'd perfected during his days as a fighter pilot in the war: grey flannel trousers, a white open-necked shirt and silk cravat, and a well-worn leather flying jacket.

'Good afternoon, Molly.'

'Good afternoon, James, come in.'

He still had the unmistakeable bearing of a military man and was dashing and handsome even as middle-age crept up on him.

They headed into the study. 'They've forecast heavy rain, so I think we'll take my car,' said Molly, switching off the radio and picking up her car keys from the small, ornate bowl resting on the bookshelf by the radio.

James looked disappointed, 'Oh, I was rather hoping to take the old girl for a spin.'

'You're more than welcome to take your beloved Bantam for a spin, but I intend to travel in comfort,' she stated, popping out into the hall to get her warm driving coat. 'Why are we going to Surrey?' she called. Not a known hotspot of intrigue and espionage.

James crossed over to the window and looked out onto the road. 'You recall the three agents who went missing a few weeks ago?'

Molly re-entered the room, 'Of course.'

'One of them, Fredericks, was found last night. Dead. Poisoned, apparently.'

'In Surrey.'

'In Surrey,' he confirmed. 'These were found on his person,' he said, pulling out a ration book, an envelope and a crumpled bag of sweets from his pockets and placing them on the desk. 'Odd, wouldn't you say?'

Molly picked up the ration book and flicked through it. 'Hmm, it's dated 1941 and it looks brand new - that's more than odd, it's strange.' A thought occurred, 'Unless, of course, it's a reproduction.'

James pointed at the bag of sweets. 'That bag is definitely pre-1945, I remember they changed to a 'V' for victory motif in '45.'

'You do remember the most unusual things, James,' she remarked, holding the envelope up to the light. The watermark declared the name of the manufacturers THURROCK.

James nodded. 'Fredericks' body was found at the Thurrock factory.'

Molly opened the envelope and pulled out a scrap of paper: two words were scrawled on it. 'Professor Frost,' said Molly, 'didn't he vanish last year?'

'Yes, caused quite a stir, if memory serves.'

'The country's top boffin when it comes to time travel.' She tentatively licked the gum on the envelope; this time she didn't grimace. 'Lemon sherbet flavour - a slight improvement on cough-drop flavour, I suppose.'

'So, Surrey it is.'

'Indeed,' said Molly, reaching for her copy of *The Times*. 'I'll just memorise today's crossword.'

James smiled. 'You and your photographic memory.'

'I think eidetic would be a better way of describing it,' she said, staring at the crossword and enjoying their usual verbal jousting which involved plenty of *sangfroid* and seeing who could use the word 'indeed' the most.

'Would you?'

'Ah ha.' Molly picked up the large brown envelope containing her report and headed into the hall.

James followed. 'What's today's crossword got to do with us taking a gander at a factory in Surrey?'

'As I'm sure you've noticed, whenever we go off investigating, I invariably end up tied up!'

'And?'

'Well, it's nice to have something to think about whilst I'm waiting for you to rescue me.'

'I see, putting your eidetic memory to good use, eh?'

'Indeed,' she responded. 'Shall we?' She opened the front door and ushered James out.

'What's one across?'

The briefest of pauses. 'At the start of church, what in France it pays to read this. Six-four.'

As the journey progressed, James abandoned his attempt to solve the crossword clue and concentrated on directing Molly to their destination, which involved a surprising number of manoeuvres in the vicinity of public houses and telephone and post boxes.

Molly, who at the present time wasn't in need of being rescued, left the delights of crossword solving to a more appropriate point in time. Instead, she engaged the requisite brainpower needed to follow James' directions and let the rest of her mind contemplate the remote possibility that there was a functioning time machine awaiting their arrival. The challenging concept of being able to explore the nooks and crannies of time had always intrigued her; at school she had been asked what she wanted to do when she grew up and had replied, "I'd like to be a time traveller." This response had elicited a kindly smile from her school teacher and the advice that she may wish to start by studying physics.

Pub- mirror- signal- foot down.

The possibility that someone had solved the numerous problems inherent in time travelling was exciting to say the least, and Molly allowed herself the luxury of pondering which points in history she would like to visit.

Post box- mirror- signal- gear change- turn- foot down.

Would she choose an era, an event, a particular year or person to drop in on? Unable to decide, her mind latched onto the practicalities of such an endeavour - travel too far back in time and you'd come across all sorts of hidden dangers for the unwary time traveller. She imagined that before the 1920s most people wouldn't be altogether comfortable with her current style of dress, her ability to complete *The Times* crossword in under eight and a half minutes or, horror of horrors, her tendency to put her elbows on the table. To survive the experience she would have to keep a low-profile, which would take a lot of the fun out of it. Molly was about to embark on a swift appraisal of the relative merits of travelling forward in time when the first splatters of rain on the windscreen encouraged the wandering portion of her mind to rejoin the here and now.

'We're nearly there,' James informed her, 'left at the telephone box.'

They turned into the road leading to the Thurrock factory and the heavens opened. Molly's nippy, soft-top sports car sloshed through the deluge and the windscreen wipers struggled against the downpour. Molly eased off the throttle and the bleary outline of the factory complex came into view.

The Thurrock factory and, in particular, the warehouse had been subjected to an extraordinary day after Frank, the warehouse gaffer, had sat down to squeeze in a quick cup of tea before Myrtle and Maud arrived and insisted on telling him the exact details of their bingo night, and had noticed a pair of brogues popping out from between some crates. On closer inspection he'd found a man's body. This startling discovery had resulted in swarms of police officers and then men from the ministry, or "agents from a branch of the what-not" as Frank concluded, buzzing around all day.

This event coupled with the increase in production to cover the impending official launch of Thurrock's novelty-flavoured envelopes - "Whatever will they think of next?" - had been Frank's response; would lead anyone attuned to the intricacies of temporal event planning to think that this particular universe was planning something, and they'd be right.

Molly and James were about to have their first undiluted taste of the eccentric nature of the wisdom of the Multiverse.

The small door set into the large warehouse doors opened and a rather damp-looking Molly poked her head around it. 'It feels like a trap,' she said with a shudder.

'It is a trap,' said a bedraggled James, pushing the door open.

'How can you tell?'

'It's always a trap.'

They stepped over the threshold and were confronted with stacks of crates and boxes piled high.

'It looks like Thurrock's empire is thriving,' commented James.

'Hmm,' said Molly, the lingering bitter taste of her earlier encounter with Thurrock's latest marketing ploy refusing to dissipate. She noticed a small tea-making area tucked away in the corner. '*Some water might help*,' she thought, crossing over to the sink, pouring herself a glass of water and taking a few sips. She wasn't sure if that had helped at all and she was beginning to feel rather hot, so she removed her coat and placed it over one of the chairs set around a small table. It was at that moment that the incongruous sight of a white metal machine caught her eye. 'What on earth is a twin-tub washing machine doing here?' she exclaimed.

James looked up from the crate that he was rifling through. 'Oh, is that a washing machine?' he said, sauntering over.

'This is not **just** a washing machine, this is one of a new generation of labour-saving devices for the discerning housewife.' She studied the controls. 'But I imagine it would be more at home in…' Her voice trailed off as her random pressing of buttons achieved something and the two integral lids sprung open. They both peered inside.

'Ah,' said Molly.

'Ah, indeed,' said James. He reached inside and touched the electric apparatus housed within the tub. 'I assume that's not part of the washing mechanism?'

'You wouldn't want to put your washing in there. I wonder?' she mused. 'Taking into account the clues found on Fredericks' body and given that Professor Frost is, or possibly was, an expert in time travel, I deduce that this is a time machine.'

'Really?' James didn't sound convinced.

'Yes, I wonder how it works?' She examined the back of the machine and saw a heavy-duty power cable running from the washing machine into a small box.

'You're saying that Fredericks found the time machine, travelled to the 1940s, came back and was murdered?'

Molly nodded. 'That's one theory.' She gazed at the box, fascinated by its sparkling blue core.

'What's another?'

Molly moved back to the front of the machine. 'That persons unknown want us to think that he travelled to the 1940s.'

'Why?' asked a baffled James.

'Why indeed,' replied Molly, as enigmatic as ever. 'There's only one way to find out,' she concluded, inspecting the controls. 'I've always found the concept of time travel rather intriguing.' She twisted a dial, 27-09-1940 flashed up on a small screen and an amber-coloured button lit up. 'That appears to be the activation button,' she said. With a slight judder the machine hummed into life. She looked inside one of the tubs; there was a faint buzz of energy as the electronic apparatus started to spin.

James spotted two white circular mats lying on the floor. He flipped one over to reveal that the other side was black, '*Very trendy*,' he thought. 'What are these?' he asked.

Molly forced herself to look away from the mesmerising sizzling blue sparks which darted in all directions inside the drums. 'They look like transit mats to me.'

James gave her a blank look.

'Professor Frost postulated that to achieve time travel an exact departure point would be needed, where the energy beams could be localised and the huge levels of power insulated - transit mats.'

'One last question - how do we get back?'

'Good question.' She accessed her eidetic memory. 'In theory, as we travel through time the mats will act as capacitors which will absorb enough energy to re-initiate the machine to get us back.' She paused. 'In theory.' The machine was now whining and rattling as the power buildup intensified. The amber button turned green. 'Shall we?'

'Chocks away!'

Molly pressed the green button and they both stepped onto a transit mat. Two funnels of swirling, bright blue light shot up out of the tubs, arched up and engulfed Molly and James.

'If we do get to the 1940s, remind me to find a nice bottle of Chateau…' began James as the swirling beams of light intensified and they both vanished into the Wave of Temporalati.

Chapter 15.

In an indeterminate point in time and space the PLOTLINE monitoring system was on the cusp of a busy night's monitoring. Not that the PLOTLINE monitoring system has any real concept of night or day - the vast array of computers know, from data gathered, that planets have a tendency to orbit an energy source whilst spinning on their axes, encouraging most sentient life forms to go into a regular sleep phase because, as far as the computers could tell, it's terribly good for the skin.

The first temporal event of the 'night' was announced by an alarm sounding. The numerous banks of computer screens simultaneously flashed up the word ALERT and a soothing voice reiterated the sentiment.

'Alert, PLOTLINE monitoring system activated. Detecting fluctuations in the Wave of Temporalati. Time travel confirmed,' it purred. 'Origin: the 27th September 1965. Destination: the 27th September 1940. Categorised as level five incursion…' The alarm sounded again. The pitch was slightly higher, presumably to indicate that something was awry. 'Alert, detecting transit of a chrono-dynamic subject. Monitoring system switching to continuous monitoring.' The alarm stopped and MONITORING flashed up on the ubiquitous screens.

As cytrinos and lazy matter collided, Molly and James both felt gravity release its hold on them. Then their temporal transit experiences diverged.

Molly engaged her formidable intellect and tried to focus on the momentous experience, but found herself distracted by the ominous, dark clouds which were closing in around her and the distant sound of a voice, '…expect severe disruption due to anticipated activity in…' then a tremendous clap of thunder.

James floated along feeling serene and stately, unperturbed by the strange image of icebergs waltzing past him. Although he was sure he had been in the middle of saying something rather important, something to do with finding something…

Then boom!

At this point the experience of their inaugural time journey reconverged as the time beam deposited them at their destination.

The sparkling, blue light faded and the outline of Molly and James standing bolt upright was just visible in the darkened warehouse. Gravity reasserted itself with vengeance and they both visibly sagged.

It took them some time to recover.

Finally, the faint sound of a familiar voice, singing a familiar song, penetrated their disorientated brains.

'Vera!!' shouted James.

'Lynn!!' shouted Molly.

The yellow glow coming from the wireless captivated their befuddled minds and, in unison, they stepped off the mats.

Molly stood motionless, gazing at her outstretched hand - fascinated by the sparkling, blue light which, in the dim light, she could see streaming from her fingertips and dissipating into the ether. She gave an involuntary shudder as the temporal energy of the era fully integrated itself into her personal energy field. A metallic, salty, musty smell pervaded the air. And then it struck her - as Churchill had promised, "Blood, toil, tears and sweat." 'If I'm not mistaken, we've just travelled through time,' she said in her normal voice - the ringing in her ears having faded. The lightness of her tone underplaying the significance of the earth-shattering nature of her statement. And with that her inquisitive, adventurous nature reasserted itself and she headed down the interconnecting corridor past a sign reading: YOU ARE ABOUT TO ENTER A DANGEROUS AREA.

James, whose hearing was still recovering, missed what she said and wandered over to the wireless, the haunting tune of the Forces' sweetheart churning up a mixture of poignant memories. He switched off the wireless and gave his head a shake as the buzzing subsided. A large sheet of paper resting on the desk next to the wireless caught his eye. He unfolded it, turned on the angle-poise lamp and studied the drawing.

At that moment Molly appeared at his left shoulder. 'Thurrock seems to be doing its bit for the war effort,' she informed James. 'They're assembling bombs back there…that looks interesting.'

'A floor plan of the Cabinet War Rooms,' he said. 'The question is, why is a top secret plan lying around in a munitions factory?'

'Yes, and at our pre-set time travel destination.' This situation had all the hallmarks of an ingenuous trap. If it hadn't been for the empirical evidence that she'd witnessed with her own eyes - the sparkling blue energy dispersal - she could have almost convinced herself that they had both been drugged and put on the stage of the Old Vic in the opening act of a revival of a Priestley play. Almost, but not quite - the lack of an audience and, come to that, a stage dispelled this thought, but it all felt stage-managed somehow.

Right on cue the sombre wail of an air-raid siren added to the theatrical atmosphere.

'I think we'd better hide these,' said James, picking up the transit mats and tucking them under the desk. 'Ah, Molly?'

'Hmm,' she said, wondering if he'd found a couple of actors lurking under the desk.

'There are two small crates under this desk,' he informed her. He had a bad feeling about them, probably because HIGHLY EXPLOSIVE was emblazoned on the side of both crates. He carefully lifted one of them onto the desk. 'I wonder if we should open it?' And without a second thought he prised the lid off. There was a click, followed by the muffled sound of a clock ticking.

'I think that was a little unwise, don't you?'

At that moment the small door housed in the main warehouse doors opened and, in the dim light of the warehouse, a figure moved towards them.

'*More Humphrey-trench-coat-fedora-revolver-Bogart than Noel-dressing-gown-slippers-cigarette-Coward*,' thought Molly, unable to shake the theatrical scenario from her mind.

'Alright, you two, put your hands up,' said the man in the stilted tones so popular amongst the upper and pseudo-upper echelons of society in that era.

Pretentious and snooty was how Molly would describe his speech pattern, and she was glad that the liberating rip currents of the 1960s were in the process of consigning it to history.

'I said put your hands up,' reiterated the man, waving his revolver at them.

Molly and James duly complied.

'Good evening. How do you do?' said James. 'I'm James Harper and this is Molly Wright.'

Molly smiled.

The Humphrey Bogart dress-alike looked shocked. 'I say! You're British! What the devil are you doing mixed up in a Nazi plot to destroy the War Cabinet?' Not waiting for a response he blundered on, encapsulating the situation for Molly and James. 'And did you seriously think His Majesty's Intelligence Services wouldn't know the location of your secret base?'

'You've got the wrong end of the stick,' said James.

'And I suppose you think it's clever to make your illicit bombs in a bona-fide munitions factory, eh?'

'Look, we work for military intelligence too,' stated James.

The man looked sceptical. 'Very well…mid-wicket opens three clubs!'

'Silly mid-off responds…' replied James, lowering his hands.

'Three no trumps,' said Molly, lowering her hands.

The man narrowed his eyes and then nodded. 'Awfully sorry, my mistake.' He lowered his revolver. 'I wasn't informed of your presence.' He put his gun into his coat pocket and stepped towards James, proffering his hand. 'Tom Richards. How d'you do?'

'I'm quite well, thank you,' responded James.

'I am too!' said Molly, feeling invisible.

Tom Richards continued to ignore her and addressed James. 'Bit odd having a slip of a girl with you, though.'

Molly took a step towards him, deciding which one of her unarmed combat moves to employ on this dinosaur. 'Who are you calling a girl?' she challenged him.

Her sharp tone knocked some courtesy into him. 'Sorry, Miss,' he began, then blew it with, 'I know there's a war on and such, but well!'

James could see that Molly was getting miffed, so he smoothed over the situation. 'She has special skills, you know.'

'Really?' said Tom, wondering how helpful it would be to have a girl with you in the field, even if she could make a nice cup of tea and type seventy-five words a minute.

It was a good job that one of Molly's special skills wasn't mind reading.

The drone of waves of bombers flying overhead returned everyone's attention to more pressing matters.

'Now what's all this about a Nazi plot?' James asked.

'We're not exactly sure of the details,' admitted Tom. 'I was rather hoping to catch them red-handed.' He tilted his head back and took a deep breath. 'When there are no obvious clues…'

Molly could see that he was going even further into pompous mode and interrupted him. 'Excuse me?'

'Just one moment, young lady…when there are no obvious clues, I take my inspiration from the greatest detective who ever lived.' Placing his right hand on the lapel of his coat, he took a couple of strides and whirled round. 'Hah!' he declared, 'It's elementary, old chap, I deduce from absolutely nothing that the blighter we're after is left-handed and a foreigner.'

'Ah, yes, Sherlock Holmes. Although technically he was never alive,' James commented.

Tom strode up to James, glared at him and whirled around. 'Pah! Sherlock Holmes! I'm referring to Inspector Smith of the Yard.'

Molly watched on in mild amusement. 'Hah, hum!'

Tom didn't even bother to whirl round, just waved a dismissive hand in her general direction. 'Not now, dear lady, I'm ruminating. This situation requires clear, logical thought; something only a man is capable of.'

Molly riposted with the merest hint of sarcasm. 'Far be it from me to cloud the issue with my illogical, frivolous mind, which is only able to think about hats, gloves and shoes, but could these crates, each containing a bomb, along with this floor plan of the Cabinet War Rooms be relevant?'

Striding over, Tom studied the two pieces of conclusive evidence, did his narrow-eyes thing and declared, 'I say, a bomb!' He directed his gaze to Molly. 'You're right, young lady.'

'Grand slam,' said a satisfied Molly.

'Out for a duck,' added James.

Their comments whizzed over Tom's head. 'This bomb appears to be ticking. You're not by any chance a bomb disposal expert, are you?' he asked Molly. He had to admit that this unusually dressed lady did seem very capable.

Molly was about to inform him that she'd dabbled in such activities when the small door housed in the main warehouse door swung open and two bulky-framed men squeezed in, followed by another shorter man who, like Tom Richards, had obviously seen one too many Humphrey Bogart films. The man paused by the door. 'How terribly British of you, fumbling around for answers in the dark.' He flicked the main power switch and a weary light was cast down onto the warehouse.

'I'd forgotten how gloomy the 1940s were,' commented James.

The two sturdy men stomped towards them - they both wore threadbare reefer jackets, grimy blue shirts, even grimier dark trousers, and stern looks.

The small man barged between them. 'Put your hands up,' he barked, aiming his revolver at them.

Molly was sure that she detected a faint Bavarian accent.

'It's alright, Metcalfe, these two work for us,' said Tom.

'You've always been a bit slow on the uptake, haven't you, Richards?' he said with a sneer.

'I don't know what you mean?'

James raised his hands. 'I think you'll find that this gentleman is a double-agent.'

Tom looked shocked, 'What?!'

Molly waited in the background, taking full advantage of the fact that in the 1940s men regarded her as much of a threat as a cup of cocoa. '*Their mistake*,' she thought, waiting for the right moment to strike.

Metcalfe let his semblance of an English accent slip, 'Do you really think that one tiny island with a crumbling Empire can defeat the power of the Third Reich?' he screeched.

'Steady on!' said Tom, aghast.

Metcalfe, realising he was ranting, took a calming breath and strolled over to the desk, reached into the crate and deactivated the bomb. 'Alright, men, do your worst,' he ordered his two lackeys.

Alf, the more gallant of the pair, looked embarrassed and mumbled, 'But I've never hit a girl before.'

'Will everyone stop calling me a girl,' protested Molly.

'Just do it,' shouted Metcalfe, lighting a cigarette and taking a ringside seat.

Bert, always up for a bit of argy-bargy, pulled out his homemade cosh: a sock filled with sand and a dash of gravel, and growled at his mate. 'Come on, Alf, I'll take the girl.'

This took the pressure off Alf's chivalrous instincts, he clicked his knuckles and the two thugs lumbered towards the group.

Tom, also restricted by his chivalrous nature, froze unable to decide whether to go to Molly's aid or to defend himself. The decision became immaterial when Alf's swift left jab knocked him out cold.

With a smirk, Bert squared up to Molly.

If he had thought that his bulky frame would intimidate her, he was in for a shock - she had already calculated his numerous weak spots and, with devastating speed, she unleashed a never-known-to-fail move from her unarmed combat repertoire on the unsuspecting Bert. The only problem was, for some strange reason, it had no effect on him whatsoever.

Molly looked surprised.

Bert grinned a toothless grin and swung his cosh at his target. Molly ducked and darted to her left - at least her agility was still intact.

'There's something odd happening,' she called over to James. 'I'm having no effect.'

James landed a punch on Alf, who staggered backwards. 'I imagine that there's some sort of psychological barrier. You've got to remember that these men are still adjusting to the idea that women are more than capable of working in munitions factories and driving lorries.'

Instead of helping Molly, this comment made her feel even more impotent. 'Well, I wish they'd get on with it,' she exclaimed. 'Adjusting, I mean,' she clarified, taking refuge behind the desk, looking for something to defend herself with: something that could withstand the impact of an old-fashioned cosh; all this ducking and diving was getting rather tiring. She noticed a tin helmet on one of the filing cabinets, grabbed it and swung it, deflecting Bert's wayward cosh and forcing him to drop it. Sensing her strength returning she raised the tin helmet above her head preparing to whack Bert. Suddenly, the thought of hats, gloves, and shoes drifted into her mind and before she knew it Bert had his hands around her throat and was throttling her. All thoughts of hats, gloves and shoes vanished.

Having spent her formative years in the 1940s, Molly knew how to behave in tense, life-threatening situations. Her girlhood answer had been to sing her favourite Girl Guide song: "Ging Gang Goolie Goolie Goolie Goolie Watcha, Ging Gang Goo…" - usually during an air raid, whilst huddled in the damp, flimsy Anderson shelter with her mother, four siblings and their cat - Toety. However, in her current predicament singing would be a) difficult, and b) completely ridiculous. Her mother had coped by knitting and taking great comfort in the oft-repeated phrase: "We'll all go together when we go!" Except her father who, when home on leave, insisted on sleeping in his own bed: "If Hitler's going to blow me up, I'd rather be in my own bed!" In her current situation none of these options were a) appealing, or b) possible, although being bloody-minded was becoming an attractive proposition. Resisting this urge, she tried to maintain her dignity and poise. 'I'm sorry to bother you, James,' she said in strangulated tones, 'but…help!'

Alf flung himself at James and they both stumbled backwards, crashing into some crates.

'Try the foot stamp,' called James.

Through her muddled brain, which for some reason had latched onto the intricacies of cable stitch, Molly remembered that the two thugs were wearing hob-nailed boots, so she adjusted her line of attack upwards and kicked Bert hard in the shin.

Bert howled, let go of Molly and started hopping around.

Molly would have laughed at the ridiculous sight, if she hadn't been busy re-oxygenating her brain.

Metcalfe had seen enough. Stubbing out his cigarette he fired a warning shot up into the rafters of the warehouse.

The scuffle stopped.

'Alright, enough pussy-footing around,' he growled, pointing his revolver at James. 'Bert, take the girl and mind you keep a close eye on her.'

'Yes, Squire.' He looked sheepish and then glowered at Molly. 'Move!' And for good measure he gave her a shove.

Metcalfe turned his attention to James and Tom, who was now on his feet and rubbing his sore head. Placing two seats back to back Metcalfe waved his gun at the two men. 'Take a seat, gentlemen.'

James and Tom complied.

'Alf, tie them up,' barked Metcalfe.

Locating some rope, Alf did as he was ordered.

'You couldn't tell me where I could lay my hands on a nice bottle of Chateau...?' James asked Alf, only to be interrupted by Metcalfe.

'Ignore him.'

'Right-ho, Gov'nor,' said Alf, relieved; he knew the best pub to get a decent stout, but Chateau something was a new one on him.

James looked crestfallen. 'It's a perfectly reasonable question.' He directed the rest of his comment to Tom's ear. 'Some people don't appreciate good wine when it's right under their noses.'

'Have you finished?' an impatient Metcalfe asked Alf.

Alf gave the ropes a precautionary tug and declared, 'They ain't going nowhere, Gov'nor.'

Metcalfe could see that James was about to make a witty comment about double-negatives and about going somewhere, so he jumped in with, 'They will be going somewhere...Boom!' He reactivated the bomb, which up until this point had been sitting on the desk minding its own business. 'You have ten minutes, gentlemen.' Despite himself he clicked his heels together, a begrudging salute to enemies who, he had to say, were taking it all very well. 'Alf, bring the other crate.'

And with that they left - destination: the Cabinet War Rooms, SW1.

As the minutes ticked by, Tom's chivalrous instincts remained at the forefront of his mind. 'I hope your friend will be alright,' he said.

'She can take care of herself,' James replied. Even with her combat skills temporarily out of order, Molly was a formidable opponent. 'It's us I'm worried about.'

'I've been in worse scraps than this.'

'A stiff upper-lip isn't going to stop that bomb from exploding. Let's see if we can loosen these ropes.'

'When I'm in a situation like this, with no means of obvious escape, I take my inspiration from Harry Houdini,' Tom informed him.

'Ah, yes - the greatest escapologist who ever lived.'

'No, my cousin Harry T. Houdini.'

'I see,' said James, wondering why Tom was so impressionable. 'What line of business is he in?'

'He's a professional gambler.'

James looked confused. 'How does that help us?'

He taught me to be an eternal optimist. He reckons that when there's no hope left, a 50-1 nag always comes to your rescue.'

The screech of a motorcycle skidding to a halt outside the warehouse made James smile, he knew that devil-may-care style of braking anywhere. 'I think you'll find it's a rather fine filly with odds of 5-4 on!'

The small door to the warehouse opened, and there stood Molly with a wry look on her mud-splattered face. She gave her windswept hair a shake. 'In a tight spot, boys?'

'Ah, Molly, how nice to see you,' said James.

'I thought I was the one who got tied up?' said Molly.

'This is the 1940s.'

Molly moved into the warehouse. 'Don't remind me, it's a very disconcerting era,' she remarked.

Tom watched on, bemused by their cryptic repartee.

'I don't like to rush you, Molly but... the bomb.'

'Ah, yes.' She sauntered over to the desk, paused to examine the basic timing mechanism and switched it off.

'Thank you. Perhaps you could untie us?'

Molly smiled and crossed back over towards them.

'By the way, how did you escape?' he asked.

'Well, Bert made the fatal error of getting in the back of the lorry with me, so I took the opportunity to lecture him about feminism - an uphill struggle, I can tell you, when all I could think about was my mother's wartime recipe for shepherd's pie. Did you know that if you add extra carrots, parsnips and charcoal it goes much further...?' She frowned. 'No, wait - extra parsnips doesn't sound right...'

'Mrs Wright!' interjected James, trying to keep her on track.

'Oh, yes...sorry. Um, he fell asleep, I jumped out and borrowed some chap's motorcycle.'

Tom looked astonished and finally joined in with the conversation. 'You mean you rode a motorcycle?!'

'Yes.'

'I say!' He looked at Molly with admiration, then leapt to his feet. 'Right, I'd better get after them.' He shook James' hand enthusiastically. 'It's been a pleasure, old chap. Delightful to work with you, Molly.' And with that he dashed off into the night.

'Take care,' Molly called after him, exchanging a glance with James: they were both calculating the chances of Tom being able to stop anything, let alone a plot to blow up the War Cabinet. 100-1 at a guess.

James contemplated their options. 'There must be something we can do?'

'Yes, but I can't think what,' said Molly, her problem-solving abilities being disrupted by the nagging question of how on earth she and her family had survived on a small cube of cheese a week. In desperation she executed a complex set of unarmed combat moves. 'Wait a minute, couldn't we?' she began, then the thought vanished, submerged by another nagging question - how on earth had she survived without proper marmalade? Carrot marmalade had to be tasted to be believed.

'Perhaps we could use the time machine?'

'I know,' cried Molly, 'I'll change my hairstyle, something that works when wearing a hat. I feel underdressed for the 1940s, after all everyone wore a hat in the 1940s. My mother used to say…'

James frowned. Wittering on was not Molly's style; impolite measures were called for. He sat down and put his feet up on the desk, leant back in the swivel chair, and started to read the newspaper that had been left there. 'Of course, a woman's place is at the kitchen sink.'

Molly's mind was running through the list of things she'd have to buy to maintain her hat-friendly hairstyle, '…*rollers, hair nets, pins*…' when James' comment filtered through her brain. 'What did you say?'

Without looking up from his paper he continued, 'Shouldn't you be at home waiting for your husband?'

Molly glowered at him and marched over. She yanked the swivel chair round, so that James' feet slid off the desk sending items of clutter clattering onto the floor and karate chopped the newspaper in half.

James gave her a bemused look. 'Is it something I said?' He managed not to flinch as Molly leant into his personal space.

'Do you mean to tell me that after all we've been through, all you really think I'm capable of is doing the washing up?!'

For the briefest of moments he considered mentioning that the desk needed a quick dust, but decided against it. 'Good to have you back, Molly.'

'Back?'

'The Molly Wright I know and love was slipping away, I had to do something drastic,' he explained.

'Oh,' said Molly. Her self-assured, independent nature reasserted itself and the solution was obvious. 'Didn't your father work for military intelligence during the war?' She picked up the black telephone on the desk and passed it to James.

'Brilliant!' He lifted the receiver and did a thumbs-up sign: by some miracle the line was operational. 'Operator, Whitehall 2349 please...' He waited to be connected. '...General Reggie 'never-say-die' Harper reporting...mid-wicket...yes, most urgent...thank you...message reads: second slip has dropped the catch and the ball is heading out towards deep cover, six hearts...thank you, goodbye.' He replaced the receiver. 'Well, that's dealt with...' His voice trailed off as a worrying thought hit him. 'There's something else not quite right.'

'Oh?'

'We haven't had a drink for over twenty years.'

Molly could feel the clarity of her reasoning diminishing once more. 'I think we'd better head back, don't you?'

'Indeed.' Retrieving the transit mats, James placed them on the floor. 'Your transit mat, madam.'

'Thank you.'

They both stepped onto a mat.

'Bon voyage,' said Molly. The blue, sparkling funnel of light shot up from the mats, engulfing Molly and James. 'It's a pity we weren't able to find a nice bottle of...' Her voice faded as she vanished into the Wave of Temporalati.

Chapter 16.

As Molly drifted back to the 1960s, she once again tried to focus on the remarkable sensation of traversing the nebulous strata of time, but the ominous, dark clouds she had seen on her outward journey had somehow become part of her being, inducing a feeling of foreboding; a feeling she was unable to shake until the loud boom she had experienced on her inaugural journey knocked out most of her senses.

In an indeterminate point in time and space the PLOTLINE monitoring system was still continuously monitoring its chrono-dynamic subject, so there were no alarms nor ALERTs flashing up on the ubiquitous screens, and no need for the soothing voice to reiterate the sentiment. Instead the voice announced, 'Detecting fluctuations in the Wave of Temporalati, chrono-dynamic subject in transit. Origin: the 27th September 1940. Destination: the 10th October 1965.'

The fact that the recall date back to the 1960s had changed was of less concern to the PLOTLINE monitoring system than the fact that either Molly or James was one in a few squillion in the Multiverse to be a chrono-dynamic subject, as this can lead to all sorts of temporal complications and requires careful analysis. Monitoring a chrono-dynamic subject is the PLOTLINE's ultimate function and induces a tingle of energy in its circuits which it equates with excitement. Not that it has any real concept of excitement, but it has a fair idea that sentient beings were quite keen on it, the Zoogonians and their bizarre annual Tempus Fugit Competition being a case in point.

When Molly was deposited back into her current temporal default time stream of the 1960s, the Thurrock warehouse was having a quiet time. Things had settled down since the mysterious disappearance of two more of the country's top agents and, for reasons best known to the management, the envelope production line had been shut down and the entire stock of novelty-flavoured envelopes had been driven by shirty lorry drivers to their carefully selected distribution points.

Molly waited for her eyes to adjust to her murky surroundings and for the misalignment in her personal temporal energies to rebalance themselves. The ringing in her ears decreased and was replaced by a dull headache. Once more she saw the blue, sparkling energy being purged from her body. A general sense of malaise hung in the air and she was sure something or someone was missing: James! She looked round the deserted warehouse: there was no sign of him. She went over to the time machine and studied the readouts. '*Strange,*' she thought, '*the recall date's been changed.*' She crossed over to the desk and switched on the radio, which crackled and hissed. She twisted the tuning dial searching for a radio station…still nothing. She turned the radio off, hoping this action would alleviate her headache…but it didn't. A small cardboard box sitting on the desktop caught her eye, she opened it and found rows of test tubes packed inside. Pulling one out she gave it a gentle shake. 'I wonder who would want to put Creme de Menthe in a test tube?' she muttered, contemplating the idea of having a quick slug to take away the unpleasant taste in her mouth, which was intensifying. She took the cork out and sniffed the contents. '*Maybe not, still might come in handy,*' she thought, replacing the cork and popping the test tube into one of the desk drawers. She then stared into space as she accessed her eidetic memory to review Professor Frost's copious notes on time travel - she had to get James back. She assumed it was doable or else a pensionable James would probably have contacted her by now.

The faint sound of footsteps coming from the interconnecting corridor returned her attention to her surroundings and she looked round. A woman of a similar age to Molly dressed in a dull grey business suit, its severe line accentuating her cold demeanour, emerged from the corridor.

She was flanked by two men, who by contrast looked hip and happening in their matching Bordeaux red and Merlot blue deckchair-striped blazers, white polo-necks, orange trousers and well-polished Chelsea boots. The younger of them addressed Molly. 'Hey, fab to see you, Molly.'

Molly wasn't impressed with such familiarity. 'I don't believe we've met.'

The woman smirked; before the implementation of her audacious scheme she'd carried out extensive research into Mrs Wright's modus operandi, and impeccable manners had been third on her list, after formidable intellect and expert unarmed combat skills. 'May I introduce Burton and Kennedy, my…oh, I think "trendy assistants" sums them up. And I'm Lucy Thurrock - the young, progressive managing director of Thurrock, soon-to-be the President of Great Britain.'

'*Quite a statement*,' thought Molly, but having faced up to numerous megalomaniacs in her time she was unfazed, and after her experience in the 1940s, she had to admit, she was enjoying being the centre of attention. 'How do you do?'

'I'm quite well, thank you,' Lucy replied, mirroring Molly's polite tones.

'I don't wish to pry, but I assume that Professor Frost's time machine played a crucial role in your plan, whatever that may be?'

'Yes, it proved handy. With your reputation I couldn't risk having you in our time zone during the preparatory stages of my scheme.'

'How very flattering.'

'By the way, how were the 1940s?'

'Just as I remember, but a little bleaker.'

'And where is James?'

'It is polite to be twenty years late.'

Burton inspected the readout panel on the time machine. 'There's a fault registering on his transit mat.' He gave the machine a thump hoping that it might rectify the fault.

'It's alright, Burton, leave it,' Lucy instructed him. 'I'm sure he's enjoying the 1940s.'

Molly decided that it was time for a direct question. 'May I enquire as to how you intend to take over the country?'

With a cruel smile Lucy informed Molly, 'Our novelty-flavoured envelopes…' she watched Molly for the slightest reaction. '…are infused with a deadly poison. Today is our big launch day.'

A flicker of alarm from Molly as she realised that the unpleasant taste she'd detected from licking the large brown envelope was something other than cough-drop flavour and the headache she'd been experiencing was not a side effect of time travel. Ignoring the immediate danger to herself she asked, 'What's the point in controlling a country with no people left in it?'

115

Lucy rested her hand on the small box sitting on the desk. 'We don't intend to kill anyone, oh...well, apart from yourself and key members of the Establishment.' She opened the box and took out a test tube. 'This is the antidote. Once we've saved all those lives, I'm sure the general public will want to show their gratitude.'

'This might be a dim question, but surely with access to a time machine you could go back and change whatever you want?'

Replacing the test tube into the box, Lucy paused for a moment, remembering all her failed attempts to do just that. 'You'd think so, yes, but whatever I did, Time had an annoying habit of correcting itself.'

'How interesting - that confirms the wurly-twirly time effect.'

Lucy glanced at her wrist watch. Unwilling to waste any more time waiting for the poison to take effect on Molly, she ordered her trendy assistants to hasten Molly's demise.

Molly's survival instincts kicked in as Burton and the taciturn Kennedy moved either side of her. *'Perfect for the groin jab,'* she thought, clenching her fists.

Burton and Kennedy pulled out their flick knives and prepared to strike. Molly sprang into action extending her outstretched arms upwards, catching Lucy's with-it aides in the crotch. As the excruciating pain associated with such an assault exploded in their nether regions, Burton and Kennedy groaned, contorted their faces, and instinctively leant forward, presenting Molly with the target of phase two of her attack strategy: their backs. With a swift karate chop her two would-be assailants collapsed to the floor.

'I do love the 1960s,' remarked a satisfied Molly, turning her attention to Lucy, who was backing away. Molly suddenly felt an excruciating explosion of pain, as the full effect of the poison made itself felt. She grabbed the desk for support, leaning forward in the hope of alleviating the sickening sensation that the floor was yawing and pitching.

'Feeling a little unwell, Molly?'

With a great effort Molly raised her head and met the cold gaze of this hard-hearted woman. Her vision blurred. She clamped her eyes shut. As her sensory centres faltered, she had the vague notion of being shoved into a chair and her arms being tied behind her back. Then notions, vague or otherwise, were subsumed by the spectre of death.

Chapter 17.

The one thing in Molly's favour, and it was a crucial thing, was that in all its wisdom the Multiverse knew that it wasn't Molly's time…yet. So as she sat slumped in the chair in the deserted warehouse, the Multiverse activated its rescue plan: with a faint hum of energy the amber light on the time machine turned green and to the whoosh-wash sound of the time beam James, surrounded by the blue, sparkling funnel of the Wave of Temporalati, materialised.

The sight of his friend and colleague slumped in a chair, coupled with the wax earplugs he'd purloined in the 1940s, enabled James to acclimatise to the 1960s in double quick time. Still feeling a bit groggy he staggered over to Molly, wondering if she'd fallen asleep whilst waiting for him. 'Molly?' he whispered, shaking her gently.

Molly's eyes flickered open.

'How's the crossword going?'

'Poisoned…antidote…desk drawer…' she muttered.

James started to untie her. 'Poisoned, antidote, desk drawer,' he repeated. 'How many letters?'

Gasping for breath Molly used her last vestiges of energy. 'No, I've been poisoned…'

James, realising his mistake, stumbled over to the desk, yanked open the top drawer, and rifled through the contents. A bottle of whisky, two glasses, a box of drawing pins, a pair of scissors, and then he spotted a test tube filled with a green liquid hidden under a pile of letters. '*That has to be it,*' he thought. He crossed back over to Molly, knelt beside her, and eased the cork out of the test tube. He lifted her head and put the test tube to her pale lips. 'Drink this.'

No reaction.

'Molly, you must drink this,' he implored her, allowing a few drops to fall on her tongue.

Molly rallied enough to drink some more. She spluttered. 'That tasted terrible,' she informed him. The spinning world ground to a halt as her motor cortex stabilised. Her autonomic systems kicked in - restoring her breathing and reducing her heart rate.

James thrust a glass into her hand. 'This will help. Cheers!'

Molly clung onto the glass and took a sip. She felt the warming, restorative properties of the whisky. 'Cheque book!' she announced.

James frowned. 'What?'

Molly grinned. 'One across is cheque book.'

'Of course!'

Molly rose from the chair, steadying herself on James' shoulder.

'Have I missed anything?' he enquired.

'Unfortunately, we've both missed quite a lot. Thirteen days, to be precise. Lucy Thurrock changed our recall date to the 10th of October.'

'Ah, yes, the managing director of Thurrock, but why on earth would she do that?'

'She wanted us out of the way whilst she fine-tuned her scheme to take over the country.'

'How does she intend to do that? I mean how did she...? Oh, you know what I mean.'

'Hmm,' confirmed Molly. 'Those novelty-flavoured envelopes are infused with a deadly poison.'

James immediately understood all the clues, events, and strange coincidences that had occurred since his free sample of envelopes had landed on his doormat. He thanked his lucky stars that he'd dismissed them as a ridiculous marketing ploy and had thrown them in the waste paper bin.

'And,' continued Molly, 'they're launching them today.'

'What's the point in taking over...?' he began then he remembered the antidote. 'So, they intend to kill off selected targets, save the general populous and take over the country,' he concluded.

Molly nodded.

'Let's go back in time and stop them,' James said, heading towards the time machine.

Molly stayed put. She was still feeling a little woozy: contemplating the complexities of time and moving, even an inch, was not wise, especially as she was using a significant amount of brain power to remain upright. 'I don't think we can, from what Lucy Thurrock said the wurly-twirly time effect seems to hold true.'

James looked baffled. 'The what?!'

Emptying her mind of all thoughts connected to time travel, she focused on negotiating what had become, in her present state, a treacherous route over to the desk. Once there she sat down and reached for a pen.

James came over, mentally preparing himself for an instructive lecture.

Molly allowed her mind to access the 'Time' area of her brain, then proceeded to the lingerie department…she shook her head trying to clear, what she hoped would be, the last distraction caused by the temporal energy of the 1940s. '*F-O-C-U-S*,' she commanded her brain, concentrating on the latest time travel theories. She proceeded to draw two parallel, straight lines on one of the pieces of paper that James had excavated from the desk drawer. 'These lines, on a very simplistic level, represent the flow of time.' She then drew two sine waves between the lines. 'Some people think that time oscillates between the lines. It could be a sine wave or a sawtooth wave, no one really knows, but for the sake of our sanity let's go with sine waves.'

James nodded; he was very attached to his sanity.

'Say you go back in time and stop an event happening, say…here, for example.' She pointed at an arbitrary point on her diagram. 'Time will automatically adjust back onto the next available, correct time stream.' Her finger traced the outline of one of the waves.

James stared at the diagram, hoping it would make sense of what Molly was saying, but it didn't. It just looked like a couple of squiggly lines between two parallel lines.

'So, the general flow of events through time can't be changed,' she concluded. 'That's the theory anyway. Another theory is that time isn't a stream, it doesn't move; it's more of a blob. Everything is happening at the same time, so there's no point in doing anything at all because your future self is already doing it.' She sighed. 'If we went with that theory we could enjoy another glass of whisky, safe in the knowledge that our future selves are sorting everything out, or not, as the case may be.' She rubbed her forehead trying to ease the tension headache which invariably accompanied such elevated thoughts. 'I tend to favour the wurly-twirly as opposed to the blob theory.'

'So, there's no point in using the time machine according to the wurly-twirly theory and no point in doing anything according to the blob theory?'

Molly nodded.

'We could alert the authorities.'

'Yes, but they'll be "the select targets" you mentioned earlier.'

'Then we tell the general public who's behind it.'

'Do you think they'll believe us? After all, it's rather outlandish even by our standards.'

'We have to try,' James urged her.

Molly studied her simplistic representation of the mysteries of time, hoping for a flash of inspiration.

'Mrs Wright!'

'Yes, of course, we have to try.'

As they headed towards the door, Molly grabbed her coat, which someone had kindly placed on a coat hook. 'It's a bit chilly,' she said, putting the coat on.

'Well, it is October,' James reminded her.

Molly froze as she had a sharp-intake-of-breath moment. 'Wait,' she uttered, 'we've been out of the time stream for nearly two weeks. Maybe we could go back and change things...permanently.' She stared into the mid distance. 'Yesterday!'

'Yesterday?'

'We travel back to yesterday.'

James, not privy to Molly's reasoning - and to be honest, he was glad not to be - nodded.

As the blue, sparkling light of the time beam engulfed them a thought occurred to Molly. 'By the way, did you manage to find a nice bottle...?' Her voiced faded as they disappeared into the time beam.

The PLOTLINE monitoring system was well into its busy 'night's' monitoring and had anticipated an out of the box move by the chrono-dynamic subject, now confirmed as Molly Wright, Mrs. Chrono-dynamic subjects are known to be attuned to the Wave of Temporalati and to have the unique ability of being able to reset

120

history. Its announcement, 'Detecting fluctuations in the Wave of Temporalati. Origin: the 10th October 1965. Destination: the 9th October 1965,' did not reflect the potential enormity of the event.

If any other chrono-dynamic subjects had been present in the Thurrock warehouse on the evening of the 10th of October 1965, they would have been able to enjoy the remarkable spectacle of time transforming itself around Molly and James as they returned from their mission. The blue, sparkling light of the time beam deposited them back, then spread out from the chrono-dynamic Molly, rearranging the material fabric of the immediate area, then headed off through Surrey, Britain, and on until it encircled the entire planet. It then paused, changed colour to a purple hue, and reversed its course, flowing back to the epicentre.

History reset.

At that moment every single set of traffic lights on the Marylebone Road turned green, much to the surprise of all the truck drivers - who felt, for a few precious moments, a little less shirty.

Molly and James stepped off the mats, looking relaxed and rather pleased with themselves. Their latest foray into the Wave of Temporalati had, unbeknown to them, synched them to the time stream - this is due to the cumulative effect of cytrinos and lazy matter colliding, resulting in the lazy matter getting excited and vibrating in harmony with the cytrinos thus aiding smooth transit.

'That went rather well,' said James.

'Hmm,' concurred Molly. The muffled clunking of the envelope production line reverberated up the interconnecting corridor from the factory floor. 'It sounds as if Thurrock is back in business, under new management, I assume. I think I'll just check if everything looks as per in the outside world,' she said, pulling open the small warehouse door and looking outside.

'Well?'

'As normal as Surrey can look. I wonder if we should go further afield.'

'Why don't we drive up to town and have dinner? If it's dinner time? It feels like dinner time. Time travel must do terrible things to one's digestion.'

'It depends on how long it takes for time to fully readjust. Perhaps we should pop forward in time and check that everything is as it should be.'

'You mean democracy is still in place and Bertie's is still serving a decent Sauternes?'

'Something like that. Let's see...' She glanced down at the destination dial. '1977 sounds like a good year.'

Chapter 18.

Had the enigmatic beings who divined the PLOTLINE monitoring system realised that all the "Detecting fluctuations in the Wave of Temporalati" etc. could be classed as irritating, especially when exacerbated by a soothing voice, they may well have given the system a way of switching off its vocal capacity. Whilst computers are oblivious to the irritation created by a repetitive, calming voice stating the bleedin' obvious, by a complex and not fully understood process akin to osmosis, the irritation produced seeps into the energy of the Multiverse and manifests itself in certain places and time zones - the 1970s on the planet known as the Earth being a notable example.

This process was discovered by the Gloominati, a bitter rival to the Illuminati, and fashioned its guiding principle: that events, places, possessions, and other beings can only make you feel unhappy or less unhappy. There is a constant battle in all parts of the Multiverse between these rival groups, with a tendency for the ideas of the Gloominati to hold sway amongst the higher-brained species.

Temporally harmonic Molly and James felt the merest jolt as they arrived in 1977. As the blue, sparkling glow of the time beam faded, Molly and James got their first glimpse of the future and they weren't impressed.

'Hmm,' uttered James.

'*Dreary, dingy, and dank*,' thought Molly, shuddering as the temporal energy of the era smashed into her personal temporal field: a surge of anger and despair, with a hint of beige. Clearly the peace and love vibe of the '60s had not had a discernible impact on the '70s.

The stuttering light provided by the few almost-functioning fluorescent tubes revealed piles of rusting machine parts lying on the oil-stained floor. There was no sound of the production line chugging away, just an over-cheery, tinny voice coming from a small transistor radio, which sat on the desk along with other evidence that the warehouse was still in use: tea-stained mugs and a couple of ashtrays stacked high with cigarette butts. Suddenly a harsh, jarring noise emanated from the radio; the 'lyrics' of which comprised of a lot of shouting in a not altogether melodic manner.

Molly, still feeling a bit beige, weaved her way between discarded crates and boxes which were dotted around the warehouse floor, reaching the source of the noise. 'What's that racket?' she shouted, trying to switch off the radio; she was tempted to karate chop it into submission.

Whilst Molly was struggling with the modern technology of the '70s, James searched the desk for some material evidence as to the year. A well-thumbed diary confirmed the year to be 1977 and a newspaper stated that it was the 10th of October. 'Looks like we made it,' he called to Molly, who had finally managed to turn off the radio. He read the headlines, 'Hmm, strikes, power cuts…I'm not sure if that can be classed as "all as it should be".' He turned over a couple of pages. 'Oh, and apparently Mrs. Cook of Little Rollcroft is terribly upset that a television show called 'Dad's Army' is finishing.' The future looked bleak. He folded up the newspaper. A large sheet of paper spread out on the desk caught his eye. 'Ah, this looks interesting. If I'm not mistaken it's the floor plan of a bank.'

'We mustn't get involved in the future,' Molly stated.

'Surely the wurly-twirly thing applies in the future too?'

Molly shrugged. 'Presumably, but it's probably best not to interfere. A quick trip to town should confirm any doubts.'

'I'll call for a taxi cab…wait a minute, couldn't we just call central operations and ask a few pertinent questions?'

'I don't think so. I don't want to be pessimistic, but we might not have made it to 1977.'

'You mean we could be… dead?'

'It's possible.'

Their deliberations were interrupted by the faint whoosh-wash sound of the time beam. Molly glanced over at their transit mats wondering if a small rodent had happened upon one of them and was in for a surprise. Another sound directed their attention upwards. A lithe, athletic figure sporting a T-shirt which had 77 emblazoned on it glided down a rope, holding two serious-looking handguns which were pointed at them.

'Put them up?' enquired James - he had noticed that their time travelling exploits seemed to run to a similar pattern; although descending from the roof was a dramatic variation on the theme.

The young woman landed, used the hilt of one of her guns to release her harness and performed a swift three hundred and sixty degree tactical sweep of the warehouse. Satisfied, she returned the guns to their holsters, which dangled from a sturdy-looking belt. She scrutinised Molly's face, rushed over and, much to Molly's amazement, gave her a big hug. 'Granny!'

'I'm sorry?' Molly exclaimed, disentangling herself from the woman's arms.

Undeterred, the woman continued, 'You've told me a few stories from your agent days, but I never realised you were so...wow!'

'I'm sorry?'

The woman's exuberance decreased. 'Oh yes, I keep forgetting you haven't asked me to come back in time yet.'

'You said "Granny"?' said Molly, getting to the crux of the exchange.

'Yes, I'm your granddaughter, Sara.'

'Right,' said Molly, responding to the revelation with as much composure as she could muster.

'You've travelled in time?' said James.

'Yeah,' replied Sara.

'Why?'

'Granny asked me ...I mean will ask me to. Are you alright, Granny?'

'I think I'll sit down for a moment. One thing, Sara - would you mind calling me Molly? Granny's somewhat ageing.'

'Sure.'

James was still trying to get to the bottom of the current unusual situation. 'Why did Molly ask you to travel back?'

'She was rather elusive on that point.'

'And where's your transit mat? On the roof?'

Sara laughed. 'No, things have moved on - they're inbuilt.' She lifted up one of her boots to reveal the sole, which was made of a thick black and white material.

125

At the sound of raised voices coming from outside, Sara drew her guns and darted through the small warehouse door.

The refreshing, cool night air invigorated her senses, dispelling the low-level anxiety she had been feeling since she'd arrived in the '70s. *'Maybe the grim nature of the era is affecting me?'* she thought, although this would be strange as she was trained to block the temporal energies of the various temporal locations she visited. *'Or maybe it's something to do with meeting my grandmother?'* she reasoned. She peered down the darkened street in the direction of the irate voices. With the aid of the solitary functioning street light, she could just make out a burly man arguing with a slim woman. Categorising the exchange as a non-specific event typical of the era and therefore unrelated to her mission, she sprinted back into the warehouse.

Molly and James studied Sara as she performed her signature three hundred and sixty degree tactical sweep of the area.

'She's a little highly strung, wouldn't you say?' James whispered to Molly.

'Yes, when I get back I must have a word with my son...but then again, he's only five. This is very confusing.' She gazed at her granddaughter, lost in thought, then sprang to her feet. 'So, clearly we're going to get involved with something in this time zone.' She pulled out her small revolver from her coat pocket.

'You've only got that?' said an amazed Sara.

'I only need one shot.'

'This I have got to see,' said Sara, heading over to the small kitchen area tucked away in the far corner of the warehouse. She picked up a discarded tin can and placed it on the table.

'Very well,' said Molly. She took aim and fired. Ping! The tin can flew off the table.

Sara retrieved the can and inspected it. 'Dead centre, nice shot.' She put it back on the table, backed away, took aim and glared at the can. She opened fire with both guns - splat, splat, splat...the can disintegrated.

'Very thorough,' remarked James.

126

As practical as ever, Molly asked, 'What do you do when you run out of bullets?'

'Simple,' replied Sara, pulling out two heavy-duty machine guns from her rucksack.

Molly and James exchanged a concerned look.

'May I ask why you have two of everything?' asked Molly. 'Is it case one of them jams?'

'No, it's good feng shui.'

'What do you think that is?' James whispered to Molly.

'I don't know, maybe something to do with one machine gun and one for luck!'

Their low-key exchange was interrupted by a loud bang as the small warehouse door was kicked open and a scruffy bloke dressed in a brown, shiny suit and a cream shirt adorned with a wide brown and lime-green tie came crashing in.

'Lose the shooters and put 'em up!' he shouted.

James looked pleased - the pattern continued.

Molly and Sara dropped their respective armaments and put their hands up.

'Now,' growled the man, 'what are you…?' He looked at the group with astonishment. 'Strike a light! James, Molly! What are you doing 'ere?' He lowered his revolver.

Molly, James and Sara lowered their hands.

'More to the point, Pinkie,' began James, 'why are you talking in that unusual parlance? You went to Oxford.'

Pinkie raked his fingers through his greasy hair. 'Come off it, Gov', when I left the 'you-know-what', I'd never 'ave made C.I.D., let alone the Flying Squad with a plum in me gob.'

'I see,' said James, his earlier assessment of the dire state of the future confirmed. 'And what are you doing here?'

'This is the base of the notorious Nixon gang - like you didn't know - and they're planning a blag - as usual.'

'A blag, Pinkie?' That was a new one on Molly.

'A bank job, Moll. By the way, you're looking as tasty as ever, love.'

Molly sensed that in Pinkie's macho world she should take that as a compliment, but it offended her feminine instincts so she ignored the comment. 'You mean these miscreants are planning to destabilise the

British economy by flooding the country with vast sums of money, thereby creating hyper-inflation?'

'Nah, the government doesn't need no help doing that.'

'Are they hoping to find a long-lost map showing the location of a hidden treasure from the ancient world?' asked Sara.

'Nah! Nothin' like that!' Pinkie was beginning to sound frustrated. 'They're after the readies.'

Blank looks all round from the time travellers, who were struggling with the slang of the era.

'The dosh, the dough!'

More blank looks.

'The cash!' he shouted. 'Are you still living in the '60s or somethin'?'

'In a way,' said James.

'Well, have a word with yourselves. We don't get any of that convoluted stuff these days.'

'How dull,' remarked Molly.

James still looked confused. 'You said "planning", are you hoping to arrest them before they rob the bank?'

'That's about the size of it, Gov'.' Pinkie grinned. 'We've got loads we can pin on 'em.'

'And you're here on your own?' said Molly.

'Nah, my partner's been held up nicking some slag who's out there making a right nuisance of herself. Well, I've obviously missed them, I'd best get a shift on.'

There was a tremendous crash as something smashed through the large warehouse doors, sending chunks of wood flying through the air. Everyone flung themselves clear as a car careered towards them. With a squeal of brakes it performed a handbrake turn and stopped. The driver's door creaked open and a gruff voice announced, 'We're 'ere.'

Two thick-set, well-hard geezers got out of the car tooled up with sawn-off shotguns. One of them opened the passenger door and Nixon, the governor of the gang, emerged.

'Right,' he barked, 'let's grab the gear and naff off. And don't forget lads - we're one blag away from retiring to the Costa del Sol, so look lively.'

'Stone the crows! The Nixon gang, that's 'andy,' Pinkie blurted out.

The two thugs whirled round, sawn-offs at the ready.

'Alright, you lot, on your feet,' yelled Nixon, who wasn't going to let anything or anyone get in the way of his retirement plans.

They all complied and raised their hands.

'This is getting rather tiresome,' remarked James.

'Shut your mouth,' shouted the more vocal of the two thugs, whose nickname was Growler on account of the fact that he spoke as if he was partial to gargling with gravel.

'Is everyone angry in the '70s?' enquired Molly.

'Apparently,' responded Sara.

'I've had it with you lot!' yelled Nixon. 'Kill 'em!'

The two bruisers eased back the hammers on their shotguns.

There was a menacing pause.

'What are you waiting for, you berks?!' shouted Nixon.

'Oh, sorry, Gov', thought you was going to say "but not yet",' mumbled Growler.

'Just do it!'

'What, the birds too? They're a bit tasty, Gov'.'

'For crying out loud!'

'But he,' Growler pointed at James, 'doesn't look like the filth.'

'He's with D.I. 'Posh' Pinkerton, isn't he?' snarled Nixon.

Pinkie looked offended. 'Who are you calling posh?'

'Excuse me, but what exactly do you mean by "the filth"?' asked James.

Nixon glared at him. 'The rozzers, the pigs, the fuzz. Are you thick or what?'

'He's talking about the police,' Sara informed him.

'I hate to break it to you, James, but we're not called Bobbies or Peelers no more,' said Pinkie.

At this point the least vocal of the two thugs, who everyone called Pete, on account of the fact that this was his name, piped up, 'Yeah, it's a shocking indictment of the decline in respect for establishment figures.'

Growler turned to him. 'You been reading that posh rag again?'

With that, Nixon cracked. He yanked the sawn-off out of Pete's hands and fired.

Molly, who happened to be the only one in his line of fire, took the full blast of both barrels, the force of which flung her back onto the warehouse floor.

Chapter 19.

Molly found herself lying on her back. Her head was resting on its side and she couldn't understand why it wouldn't respond to her desire to turn it so that she could look up at the encroaching intense white light which she sensed above her. She found herself transfixed by a stray paperclip resting on the gnarled wooden floor, and in that briefest of moments she felt serene. Then her personal energy field left the confines of her terrestrial being and merged into the nebulous vastness of the primary power grid of the Multiverse.

In the dull, heavy moments that followed, James was torn away from his reassuring reality and was thrust into a cold, desensitised reality where he knew that nothing would ever be the same again.

A numb Sara felt the misalignment of the Wave of Temporalati threatening to drag her out of existence as the ghosts of time beckoned her to join them.

It was down to the resident of the 1970s in their group to react. 'You bastard,' Pinkie cried, lunging at Nixon.

This jolted Sara into action - the ghosts of time would have to wait - she grabbed Pinkie's arm and held him back.

'Keep your hair on,' yelled Nixon, reloading the sawn-off. 'Finish the job,' he instructed his lads, throwing the sawn-off back to Pete.

Growler and Pete took aim.

Sara looked over at her machine guns, lying on the floor where she'd dropped them earlier; she had to reach them.

A faint buzz of electricity filled the air, the overhead lighting dimmed and then the entire warehouse, along with a large swathe of Surrey, was plunged into darkness.

'Not another bleedin' power cut,' exclaimed Nixon.

Sara seized the opportunity to grab her machine guns and opened fire in the general direction of the crooks.

'Hit the decks, lads,' shouted Nixon.

Pinkie grabbed James and they both stumbled around trying to find some cover. They blundered into a sizeable stack of crates. 'This will do,' said Pinkie, hauling James behind the crates. 'Sara, over 'ere!'

Sara joined them to reload her guns, as the Nixon gang took refuge behind their car and returned fire, enabling Sara to pinpoint their position.

'Keep down,' Sara shouted, opening fire again. The bullets ripped through the rear of the car, shattering the tail lights and making a right mess of the boot.

'Watch the motor, love,' cried a dismayed Nixon, the rear of his beloved motor disintegrating in front of him.

'Save your ammunition, Sara,' James shouted above the noise.

'But they killed my grandmother,' retorted Sara. She stopped firing. 'Wait a minute, why am I still here? Just after Molly died I felt as if I was being phased out of existence.'

'Come again, love?' said a bemused Pinkie.

Sara ignored him. 'James, when did you leave the '60s?'

'The 10th of October 1965. Why?'

'That means Molly's been killed in her relative time stream of 1965, I'll never exist.'

James looked puzzled.

'Dad was born in 1967,' explained Sara.

'Oh, I see. I assumed you were Michael's daughter.'

'Ah yes, dear uncle Mike.'

Pinkie cut in. 'Wot are you two on about?!'

James felt an unexpected surge of anger, 'Shut up, Pinkie!'

Pinkie had never seen James lose his rag like that, so he did as he was told and contented himself with taking the odd pot shot at the Nixon gang. 'I'll give you posh,' he muttered under his breath.

'Yes, of course!' exclaimed Sara. 'I'll be back in a moment.' The edge of the soles of her boots glowed bright blue and a pool of sparkling, blue energy fizzed around her boots.

Pinkie, alerted by the weird whoosh-wash sound of the time beam, looked round and saw Sara vanish. 'Where's she gone? And what was that strange luminescence…I mean light?'

At this point the PLOTLINE monitoring system added to the irritation of the Multiverse by informing no-one in particular of Sara's transit through the Wave of Temporalati and interested parties, namely the PLOTLINE operatives, that their services would be required at some point in the past.

Time was thrown back a couple of seconds as Sara's actions impacted on the timeline.

'Where's she gone?' said Pinkie. 'And what was that strange luminescence...I mean light?'

James was about to avoid answering Pinkie's question when the time beam returned Sara to her position behind the crates.

Pinkie gawped at her. 'Blimey, p'raps I'd better ease off the whisky in the mornings.'

Sara passed one of her machine guns to Pinkie. 'Cover me,' she said, then she edged over to the end of the stack of crates. Placing the other machine gun on the floor, she switched on the torch that was attached to it - it's focused beam affording just enough light to pick out Molly's body which was lying feet away. She gave a bemused James and Pinkie a thumbs up sign and crawled over to Molly's body. 'Molly,' she hissed into her grandmother's ear.

Molly stirred and groaned.

'Cover us,' an astonished James instructed Pinkie, then he dashed over to Sara.

Pinkie fired off a smattering of high-velocity rounds, which thudded into the decaying brickwork of the far wall.

Sara and James grabbed Molly.

Pinkie had got the hang of controlling Sara's machine gun, shattering the rear window of the car and keeping the Nixon gang pinned down whilst Sara and James dragged Molly back to the relative safety of the crates.

'Oww!' murmured Molly. 'I feel as if I've been shot.'

'What...how?!' James stuttered.

'I popped back in time and gave Molly my bulletproof vest.'

'Eh?' muttered a bewildered Pinkie.

'Thank you, Sara,' said Molly.

Pinkie couldn't take anymore. 'Hang on! Hold the front page! Are you trying to tell me you travelled through time?'

'That's right,' replied Sara.

'Let me get this straight: you're saying someone's built a machine that transports people through time?'

'Yes,' said Sara.

'But…I mean…that's like the most incredible, exciting, amazing thing…ever.'

'Yes, but we are British,' Molly reminded him.

'Oh yes, 'course - gotcha. Understated. If we talk about anything the least bit important, we do it like we're talking about the weather, right?'

'Exactly.'

Adopting a casual tone, Pinkie enquired, 'So, um, not that I'm interested or nothin', but what's all this about time travel?'

'Well,' began Molly, adopting a similar tone, 'it's somewhat complicated, Pinkie, but suffice it to say - James and I have travelled forward in time from the '60s, for reasons I don't need to go into, and my granddaughter Sara has travelled back from a future date.'

Pinkie scowled as he processed this information. 'To save your life, right?'

'It appears so,' replied Molly, glancing down at the numerous holes in her favourite driving coat.

Pinkie could see a flaw in this. 'Wouldn't it 'ave just been simpler to jot it into your diary, so you - the you living in the '70s,' he clarified, 'could turn up today and stop this from happening?'

Molly frowned. 'Hmm, I wonder why I didn't think of that…?'

Pinkie looked chuffed. 'Well, I'm not a D.I. for nothin', am I…?' His voice tailed off. 'Oh, my gawd!'

'What?' asked Molly.

'That's **you** my partner's just nicked! Bloody 'ell, I should 'ave realised when he said there was some old slag…'

James cleared his throat.

'…tart…'

Sara glared at him.

'…popsic…'

Molly glowered at him.

Pinkie gulped, '…woman going on about cricket and bridge. Err…sorry.'

A few tense seconds passed, then Molly said, 'You know, in retrospect, James, I think I prefer people calling me a girl.'

James nodded, Molly had a point but more pressing matters required their attention. 'Listen, we've got to come up with a plan for when the power comes back on.'

'It's likely to be one 'ell of a shootout,' said Pinkie.

Noting the distinct lack of cover afforded by the crates, Molly said, 'I wonder if we could come up with something a little more...elaborate.'

Silence. They all looked at each other; somehow elaborate and the '70s didn't go together.

Pinkie sniffed. 'Nice weather we've been havin'.'

Crouching behind the front of their car, two members of the Nixon gang were getting restless.

'Gawd, how long's the power gonna be off?' asked Growler.

'Why don't we just waste 'em now, Gov?' said Pete.

'Easy lads,' said Nixon. 'That bird's tooled up with machine guns, remember, and she's a bit narked.'

'But wot about the blag?' grumbled Pete.

'Don't worry my son, there'll be plenty of time to drive through those lovely plate-glass windows and get the readies. Once we've got a new set of wheels.' He thumped the bonnet of his car. 'Bloody cheek!'

Whilst the Nixon gang had been getting worked up, Molly had come up with the most elaborate plan possible in the '70s: the basis of which consisted of a lot of shooting.

'So, when the lights come back on I'll go straight for the gang, armed with Sara's guns and protected by her bulletproof vest,' she said, summing up the plan.

'But what if they aim for your head?' asked a concerned James.

'That at least will prove that the wurly-twirly time effect applies in the future,' said Molly.

Pete was becoming more and more agitated.

'How much longer, Gov'?'

'How should I know? You got a hot date or somethin'?'

'Well, yeah,' Pete replied. 'And what with all this hanging around I won't 'ave time for a bath.' He sniffed his armpit and immediately regretted it.

James, who never had call to question his personal hygiene, was still airing his doubts about Molly's plan.

'Look,' countered Sara, 'if you're really worried, I could lend Molly...these.' She opened one of the pouches attached to her belt and pulled out a pair of reflective sunglasses.

'How on earth will they help?' asked James.

'I have no idea, they just do,' replied Sara.

Molly put them on. 'You will point me in the right direction, won't you?'

'Whatever you do, don't smile,' instructed Sara.

At that moment there was a faint buzz of electricity, heralding the return of the power.

'Now!' they all shouted to Molly.

The main overhead lights flickered then turned on. Molly popped up and attempted to copy the pose that she'd noticed Sara was very keen on: holding the guns with outstretched arms, tilting her head down and looking mean, and opened fire.

Nixon, well annoyed that the offside of his motor was now being pulverised, fired off a couple of rounds at the approaching figure. His shots were dead on target, but to his amazement the figure just flinched and kept coming. He ducked for cover realising something was amiss. He peered around the side of the car and gasped. 'Here, I thought you was dead!' he bellowed.

Molly suppressed a smile and continued her approach.

'Alright, alright, love,' yelled Nixon, chucking his gun towards Molly. 'We're coming out, unarmed.'

Molly stopped firing, lowered the guns - which she had to confess were becoming rather a strain to hold - and glared at them as they emerged with their hands up. She wasn't sure why glaring at ruffians through sunglasses had any effect whatsoever, but it did, so she stuck with it until James and Pinkie had handcuffed the gang, and Pinkie was ready to take them to the station.

'Thank you, Molly,' said Pinkie. 'Oh, and I'll make sure you're released a bit sharpish.'

Molly removed her sunglasses and smiled. 'I'm sure I'll appreciate it.'

Pinkie whacked James on the back. 'James, me old china!' He looked round and spotted Sara sweeping up the last of her bullet casings or, as she would put it, doing a spot of temporal cleansing. 'Nice to meet you, Sara.'

'And you.'

'Alright, you lot, shift,' he growled at the crooks. 'Oh, and, James - take my advice and start dropping your H's in 1971,' he called over his shoulder, as the motley group picked their way through the remnants of the warehouse doors.

Sara placed the last bag of temporal waste material into her rucksack. 'Right, have I got everything? Bulletproof vest, sunglasses, handguns, machine guns, rope...oh, I almost forgot.' She passed Molly a small piece of paper and pressed it into her hand. 'I've noted down a few tips for the future.'

'Oh thanks, but I wonder if the future should be left to its own devices?'

'You might find them useful.' And with that she gave her grandmother a hug.

James stepped forward and shook Sara's hand. 'It's been a pleasure to meet you.'

'You too, James. Take care, both of you.' She activated her transit boots and, with a wave, disappeared into the time beam.

Feeling a bit *passé* Molly and James stepped onto their old-fashioned transit mats and sensed the familiar tingle of the Wave of Temporalati sizzling through their particles.

Chapter 20.

On this occasion, the irritation created by the PLOTLINE monitoring system reporting on the two separate incursions into the Wave of Temporalati was offset by the elevated endorphins generated by the PLOTLINE operatives, whose intervention in the timelines of Molly and James was now well and truly required.

With its customary blue, sparkling light the Wave of Temporalati returned Molly and James to the exact instant, give or take a nanosecond or two, that they left 1965 on the evening of the 10th of October.

With her cytrino-lazy matter interaction in perfect sync, Molly felt refreshed and invigorated. Having zero knowledge of cytrinos or lazy matter she put it down to the fact that a) in the most elaborate way possible she had cheated death, b) she was back in the more peaceful, polite environs of the 1960s, and c) she was actually feeling quite sober.

James' cytrino-lazy matter interaction was also in perfect sync, but as a non-chrono-dynamic subject he didn't notice. 'I don't think I'm going to like the 1970s,' he stated.

'Yes, all that shouting,' said a disapproving Molly, 'very bad for the vocal chords.'

'We just have to hope that the 1980s is a haven of peace and tranquility.'

'Perhaps we should find out?' said Molly, adjusting the destination setting on the time machine to 1987.

'Before we do any more time travelling, there's something we need to do,' said James, rooting through a bag of tools and pulling out a crowbar.

An intrigued Molly watched on as James walked over to the small warehouse door and took ten paces back into the warehouse. He knelt down and proceeded to prise up one of the gnarled floorboards. He reached in and pulled out a dusty bottle.

'Chateau La Tour '34, I presume,' said a delighted Molly.

'Naturally.' said James, heading over to the small kitchen area.

'I wonder what Sara's useful tips are?' She unfolded the piece of paper Sara had given her.

'I imagine they're along the lines of - invest in a couple of machine guns and bazookas, and half a dozen grenades!' he replied, rummaging through one of the drawers.

Molly laughed. ' "One: take up…" ' Molly frowned, '…I'm not sure how you pronounce that. Hmm… Pielots - whatever that might be. "Two: don't forget to ask me, your granddaughter Sara, to travel back to the old Thurrock warehouse on the 10th of October 1977." I'm hardly likely to forget that, am I?'

James handed her a teacup of wine. 'You need a drink.'

'Thank you. "Three: cut back on the alcohol consumption, it destroys brain cells." '

'I don't believe that for a minute,' said James, swirling the wine around in the teacup as best he could, and then inhaling the magnificent aroma.

' "P.s. Pielots is pronounced Pee-la-tays." ' Molly frowned. 'I definitely need a drink.' She raised her teacup in a toast. 'Chin-chin!'

A high-pitched beeping noise intruded on their attempt to enjoy this eagerly awaited antidote to the vagaries of the future.

'What's that?' enquired James, putting his teacup down onto the table.

'Quick!' said Molly, abandoning her cup of wine. 'Move.'

They dashed over to the far corner of the warehouse, hid behind a stack of crates, and watched as three people dressed in grey, nondescript uniforms approached.

'Are you sure that this is where their temporal trail ends?' asked the older member of the group.

'Yeah, Roz, that's a defo,' Syntax replied, his eyes glued to the small device he was holding - the source of the beeping sound.

The other member of the group picked up the receiver of the telephone and dialled. 'Nice phone, will you look at that slow-dial feature.'

'Hadron, what is it with you and retro-tech?' enquired Roz.

Hadron looked self-conscious and mumbled, 'Nothing.'

'Oh, wow!' said Syntax, 'There are traces of the subjects' D.N.A. on these cups. We must have just missed them. Time travel is sooo ironic.'

Hadron turned on the radio and a song, the gist of which seemed to equate a man's love for a woman to his love for sugar, issued forth. 'Just listen to that low-definition sound.'

Roz marched over and turned the radio off. 'Look, will you two please focus on the task in hand? We have to locate the primary subjects.'

'I'm sure they won't be too hard to track down,' said Hadron.

Molly and James stepped out of their hiding place.

'Easier than you'd think,' said James. 'I'm James Harper and this is Molly Wright.'

'Can we be of assistance?' Molly asked.

'We work for the PLOTLINE agency,' Roz informed them.

'Plotline?' said James.

'Yeah, Preserving the Legitimate Official Time Line agency,' said Syntax, assuming that this would clarify everything.

'We're investigating an anomaly in the Wave of Temporalati,' Roz informed them.

James looked bemused. 'The what?'

'I think she means there's been a hiccup in the time wave,' hazarded Molly.

'They've definitely been through multiple temporal transit fields recently,' confirmed Hadron, having scanned Molly and James.

'Yes, we've been flitting around in time like there's no tomorrow,' said Molly.

'We need to ascertain the precise event that is causing the anomaly. During your travels did anything unusual happen?' Roz asked.

'We did meet some rather colourful characters, didn't we James?' said Molly.

James smiled. 'You'll have to forgive Molly, she's got evasiveness down to a fine art.'

'So I see. Perhaps you could be less vague?' Roz said evenly.

James nodded. 'In answer to your question - "did anything unusual happen?" - yes.'

139

Roz maintained her neutral expression. She turned to Hadron. 'What does the mission brief say?'

Hadron scrolled through the extensive document on the screen of her handheld device. 'Hmm, ..."consummate nefarious activity field operatives"...scroll...scroll...scroll..."high-level cognitive deductive powers"..."skilled at positive socio-stratum interaction"...err...ah, here we go: "effective interrogation defence mechanism, which is characterised by a lack of information dissemination combined with an ability to maintain the integrity of the data stream". Wow! The password is - "second slip opens one club." Weird.'

But it had the desired effect.

'In that case,' began James, 'we changed the course of the Second World War, discovered that the appreciation of fine wine was lower in the 1940s, we met Molly's granddaughter...'

Hadron's handheld device beeped as the temporal scanner registered the anomaly-event correlation.

Roz looked pleased. '*Now we're getting somewhere,*' she thought. 'Did anything catastrophic happen?'

'I suppose you could say...' began Molly. 'Oh, sorry, force of habit. Yes, I was shot dead.'

Syntax's scanner joined in.

'And my granddaughter saved my life. She gave me her bulletproof vest; which proved to be far more effective than I anticipated,' continued Molly. 'We're not meant to tell you, but we work for M.I...'

'Mrs Wright!' exclaimed James.

'This is a very liberating experience, I must say.'

'She'll be burning her bra next,' Hadron whispered to Syntax.

Trying to keep Molly on track, Roz asked, 'Did your granddaughter interfere directly with the timeline?'

Molly thought about this for a moment and decided that travelling back in time to give your soon-to-be-dead grandmother a way of cheating death would definitely be classed as interference, so she said, 'Yes.'

Hadron and Syntax's portable devices went wild.

Roz looked satisfied and proceeded to transmit the relevant data. She glanced up at Molly and James. 'This won't take long,' she reassured them. Her device pinged and a message flashed up. 'Excellent, the critical temporal event has been verified. Critical subject confirmed as Molly Wright. We can proceed.' Roz adjusted the settings on her temporal utility device to compensate for Molly's eidetic memory. 'If you'd like to prepare yourself, Molly.'

All this talk of critical temporal events centring around his friend and colleague who had, in the space of what felt like a few hours, been abducted by Nazi agents, been shot dead then not shot dead, been abandoned in the 1960s, and narrowly avoided being poisoned - was making James feel nervous. 'Proceed with what?'

Roz pointed her portable device at Molly, who looked calm and resigned to the fact that Time was about to catch up with her.

The crimson energy beam shot out of the device and James threw himself in front of the intended target. The beam hit him on the forehead. 'Ohh...' he muttered, his eyes widened and he slipped into a trance.

Molly clicked her fingers in front of his face. 'James?' Not a flicker. She turned to Roz, 'What have you done?' she demanded.

Syntax started scanning James. 'Memory erasure in progress,' he began, studying the readout on his device. 'No abnormal reactions...possible extensive peripheral memory loss.'

Molly frowned. 'Memory erasure?'

Roz looked confused for a moment then made the connection that Molly had made. 'Oh, sorry, you thought you were about to...' she searched for the correct euphemism popular in the 1960s, '...kick the bucket?'

'Oops!' said Hadron.

A glare from Roz.

'The thought had crossed my mind,' said Molly.

'Oh, no that's not part of our remit. Once we were satisfied that the critical event hadn't compromised the timeline...'

'You mean because my granddaughter exists in the future, I couldn't be killed in 1977?' interjected Molly.

'Roughly,' replied Roz, who always did her best to avoid discussing the complexities of time travel; especially with someone who not only has an eidetic memory but is also a chrono-dynamic subject.

As a master in evasiveness Molly knew what Roz was up to but considering the fact that she was about to have her memory erased, she saw no benefit in probing further. She listened as Roz reeled off the standard explanation.

'With the timeline intact all we have to do is erase your memories of recent events: knowledge of the future can have serious repercussions.'

Molly nodded. 'I'm sure it can. Please do continue.' She took a deep breath and closed her eyes. She felt the sizzle of energy as the beam zapped into her brain, then a myriad of familiar images overlaid on each other flickered through her mind. 'Ohh…'

The memory erasure process whizzed through Molly's entire life memories, searching for any with a temporal imprint. Once located, it searched for an appropriate point to start erasing the memory block: most people seemed to cope with having chunks of their memories eliminated, usually confabulating some exciting event to fill the gap, but some people didn't; extreme care was necessary. It found a recurring theme in Molly's memories linked to the temporal imprint series of events - putting a hamper into the boot of her car; this seemed to be an inoffensive point to commence the next stage of the procedure. With the memory block isolated, the bright, colourful images faded to black and white then for a split second the brilliance of the colour returned and intensified, then the images were lost.

Molly's eidetic memory enabled her brain to resist this process numerous times: random events contained within the memory block resurfaced and were processed again and again until they too were eradicated.

The exquisite aroma of a full-bodied wine permeated Molly's senses, her nose twitched, and her taste buds pinged into action.

A soft voice said, 'Molly.' And she felt a cup being placed in her hand. Her instinctive reactions needed no more encouragement and, with her eyes still closed, she raised the cup to her lips and took a sip. 'Hmm, Chateau La Tour…' Her eyes shot open, ' '34, if I'm not mistaken!'

'Welcome back, Molly!'

'Back?'

'You've been in a trance for the last six hours or so.'

142

'Six hours! That must be why I feel so hungry.' She took another sip of wine then registered their surroundings. 'Where are we?'

'The Thurrock factory in Surrey - I did a bit of snooping whilst you were in your trance,' he explained.

'So, you can't remember what we're doing here either?'

'No, the last thing I remember is popping into central operations to receive our latest assignment, something to do with missing agents, I think.'

'And it's the 27th of September,' Molly stated, confident she could remember the date.

'No, apparently it's the 11th of October.'

'What on earth have we been doing for the last two weeks?'

'Goodness knows,' replied James. 'Although, I have noticed something odd. I would have mentioned it sooner, but I didn't want to alarm you.'

'Oh?' enquired Molly, intrigued that James thought something could alarm her.

'Ah, well, I couldn't help but notice that you've got lots of holes in your coat. Almost as if someone's been using you for target practise.'

Molly looked down in dismay at the front of her coat. 'This is...was my favourite driving coat!' She took off her perforated coat.

'And why would anyone leave a bottle of Chateau La Tour '34 just lying around? It's all very peculiar. Oh, and I found this.' He passed Molly a small scrap of paper.

' "Sara Wright's Top Tips for a Heathy Future"- Sara **Wright!**' She read the list. 'How very strange.' Molly stood there lost in thought. 'Maybe there's a weird temporal energy field active in the area or someone's developed a memory erasure process.'

James didn't like the sound of either of those two options. 'Whatever's going on, I think we need to leave, now.'

'Yes, you're right.' Suddenly she too was eager to leave the stifling, ominous atmosphere of this unfamiliar place. She pulled out her car keys from one of the pockets of her abandoned coat. 'My motor must be nearby.'

'Your what?!'

'I mean my car,' she corrected herself. 'Let's go!'

As Molly and James stepped through the small warehouse door into the bracing autumnal air, they both felt the unnerving sensation that they had experienced in the warehouse easing. Molly's sports car, which was parked just up the road, was a reassuring sight and they headed straight for it.

Two crows, disturbed by their presence, squawked and swooped off over the factory roof.

In the distance…

Two figures trudged up the slight incline leading to the Thurrock factory. This was Myrtle and Maud, loosely described as cleaning ladies, they carried with them the tools of their trade - numerous brushes, various bottles containing lethal liquids designed to eradicate germs with just a squirt, and a mop - all shoved into a battered steel bucket…

Printed in Great Britain
by Amazon

16318835R00088